DIAMOND EYES

Previous Nudger mysteries by John Lutz:

Nightlines
Right to Sing the Blues
Ride the Lightning
Dancer's Debt
Time Exposure

DIAMOND EYES

JOHN LUTZ

ST. MARTIN'S PRESS

NEW YORK

Library of Congress Cataloging-in-Publication Data

Lutz, John
    Diamond Eyes / John Lutz.
        p.   cm.
    "A Thomas Dunne book."
    ISBN 0-312-05074-7
    I. Title.
    PS3562.U854D53   1990   90-36141
    813'.54—dc20   CIP

First Edition: December 1990
10 9 8 7 6 5 4 3 2 1

For Jeff, Wendy, and Ben

"Stones of small worth may lie unseen by day,
But night itself does the rich gem betray."
—*Abraham Crowley*
Davideis

"The lively diamond drinks thy purest rays."
—*Thomson*
The Seasons

DIAMOND EYES

1

"Yellow," Nudger mumbled to himself as he strode through the airport terminal's pneumatic glass doors. "I'm parked on the yellow level." It was easy to forget where you left your car in the airport's vast and multilayered garage. The doors hissed closed behind him.

He made his way through the maze of baggage carousels, shops, snack bars, and glass-encased displays to the corridor leading to Gate 43, where TWA Flight 109, bringing Danny back from visiting his cousin in Phoenix, was due to arrive in less than five minutes. He passed through the metal detector without incident, though the uniformed female security guard glared at him, and walked five miles to the gate. Seemed like five, anyway. Lambert St. Louis International Airport was laid out for Paul Bunyon.

Nudger disdained the use of the People Mover, which was a sort of long, flattened escalator that went neither up nor down, only forward. Standing on the thing saved some effort and massaged the soles. But the people moving alongside the People Mover were moving faster than the people moving on the People Mover. Of course, you could walk on the People Mover, but that meant bumping and being bumped by the carry-on luggage of the people properly standing on the People Mover's right, and jostling the people improperly standing on the People Mover's left. They wouldn't move.

Nudger finally reached Gate 43. He stood and craned his neck before the rows of monitor screens listing arrival times. Danny's flight was going to be fifteen minutes late. He had plenty of time after all. As he watched, the screen flickered and the numbers changed. Oops! Flight 109 was going to be half an hour late. Airlines, like medical doctors, had little regard for their clients' time.

Sighing, Nudger turned away from the monitors and noticed a nearby snack shop. He walked over and paid too much for a Diet Pepsi in a paper cup, but it had cracked ice, which he preferred over cubes, so he didn't feel too bad about the price.

He coaxed a *Post-Dispatch* newspaper from a balky yellow vending machine that snapped shut and almost cut off his hand at the wrist, as if it wanted the paper back. Then he returned to Gate 43 and settled into one of the many beige plastic chairs facing the wide windows that looked out on the runways and several angled TWA planes being fueled and loaded with luggage. Workers, some of them in coveralls despite the heat, bustled about. Blocky little vehicles, dwarfed to toy size by the aircraft, maneuvered and darted across concrete vistas as if afraid for their mechanical lives. The red-and-white planes glistened in the July sun, and the glare from outside made Nudger's eyes ache. At least it was cool in the airport; not a bad place to wait. He settled down as comfortably as possible in a tiny molded chair to read the paper.

Nudger tore out a Hardee's fast-food coupon from an ad printed in the paper, then he worked his way through national crime and corruption on the front page to local crime and corruption on the inside pages. He'd finished his Pepsi and was munching cracked ice as he read Bill McClellen's column. McClellen was a dandy columnist; he had a feel and compassion for the common man without being a sentimentalist. Today's column was about discrimination against a Vietnamese immigrant's ethnic restaurant on the city's south side. A smart-ass alderman was involved, giving the woman the bureaucratic runaround. By the time he finished reading the column, Nudger was mad. He was himself ready to gallop to the rescue of some unfortunate and right a wrong.

He set the paper aside so his fluttering stomach would calm down, then munched an antacid tablet as he squinted out at a huge 747 touching down. Puffs of dark smoke sprouted behind the landing gear tires as they kissed concrete. Danny's flight? Nudger rotated his wrist and glanced at his watch. Still too early. People seated close to nearby Gate 42 stirred, anticipating meeting incoming passengers. No one stood up, though. It really didn't do much good to watch for a landing TWA plane; this was the TWA hub airport, the hive, and hundreds of flights a day arrived and departed like industrious red-and-white bees.

Nudger wondered how Danny's visit with his cousin in Phoenix had gone. They hadn't seen each other since they were kids, Danny had said two days ago over a Dunker Delite. Danny owned and managed Danny's Donuts, the doughnut shop located directly below Nudger's second-floor office in Maplewood. The Dunker Delite, a formless sort of sugared half glazed, half cake doughnut, was his specialty. It was short on nutritional value and long on cholesterol. It tasted that way, too, though Nudger would have been the last to say so and injure Danny's sensitive psyche. He and Nudger were close friends, which worked out well, as Danny often acted as Nudger's pseudoreceptionist, not to mention lookout and co-conspirator. The downside of the shop's proximity to the office was that Nudger often smelled like a doughnut. That didn't drive women wild.

His right leg was going to sleep; he gingerly shifted his weight. His pelvis was almost numb from contact with the hard plastic chair. He thought about standing up, but swiveled his body to the side instead, lifting his left buttock off the unyielding surface.

That was when he noticed the crying woman.

She was one of maybe twenty people seated in the waiting

area. A small woman with short blond hair, wearing a white sleeveless blouse and a dark skirt with blue high-heeled shoes. She was clutching a wadded white tissue in a red-nailed hand. Nudger noticed she had trim ankles and a runny nose. Not crying, she would be very attractive.

She seemed to sense his eyes on her, the way women do, and pressed her knees together so tightly the flesh around them became pale and mottled. After dabbing at her reddened eyes with the tissue, she used it to give her nose a swipe. She sniffled and bowed her head. Mucus misery, all right. He wondered why.

She had no carry-on luggage around her, so Nudger figured she was waiting for someone, maybe on the same flight as Danny's. But more likely it was one of the other flights. There were half a dozen gates—which were really no more than doors—served by the same waiting area. Nearby were a couple of counters with computers, behind which stood airline agents who assigned boarding passes as departure times neared. No one was checking in at either counter right now, so the woman appeared to be alone and not waiting for a traveling companion who was arranging for boarding passes. There was no sign of a ticket protruding from pocket or purse. She was a St. Louisan, then.

Stop being a detective, Nudger admonished himself.

Huh? He was always a detective, whether his nervous stomach liked it or not. It was his curse and his meager means of support.

He got up and walked over to the woman. She didn't look up at him. This was awkward. He said, "Listen, whatever's wrong, if there's anything I can do to help . . ."

She glared at him, her blue eyes brimmed with tears. "Nobody can help." The pain in her voice was almost palpable.

He sat down next to her. "Hey, I've heard that before. Sometimes it's true, sometimes not. But whoever says it always *thinks* it's true. At the time, anyway. So maybe you wanna talk about it."

She said, "Go away."

Well, that was fairly plain.

Nudger stood up and drew his wallet from his hip pocket. Got out one of the three dog-eared business cards he carried tucked behind his driver's license, and held it out for her. "Take this, please. In case you need my kind of help."

She accepted the card and held it at arm's length, as if she needed glasses to read but didn't want to bother putting them on. Then she listlessly laid it on the chair where Nudger had been sitting. "Just go away."

He did. Returning to the chair where he'd read the paper, he picked up the section with the comic strips and tried to read it. Even *The Far Side* failed to give him a chuckle. He gave up on the effort and laid the paper back down.

Several people in the waiting area turned their heads to stare out the wide, bright windows. A young woman led her two small children over to stand close to the glass. Pointed out at another 747 dropping toward the runway. There were the puffs of black smoke rising behind the plane's tortured tires. One of the kids, the boy, began yammering something Nudger couldn't understand and jumping up and down with excitement. Probably Daddy was on the plane, bringing home a souvenir T-shirt.

The aircraft disappeared from view for about five minutes, then taxied into sight and veered toward the deplaning area. Sunlight glanced blindingly off its smooth fuselage; shimmering heat fumes danced like wild spirits behind its powerful engines.

Nudger sat forward suddenly. Hey, that was incredible! His eyes saw but his mind rejected.

A brilliant orange flower was blooming behind the plane's swept-back wing, just above where it joined the fuselage. He could see, quite clearly, the pale face of one of the passengers pressed to a window, watching what he was watching, so it must be real.

The orange flower blossomed with astonishing rapidity. Then everything outside the window was a blinding orange. A roar shook the waiting area. Shock and heat radiated through the wide expanse of glass. The floor sprang to life and vibrated.

Nudger had stood up without realizing it, his right arm flung across his face. He was barely aware of people screaming, of the crashing, musical sound of shattering glass, a melody of terror.

It all seemed to be happening slowly and at a great distance, in another place and to other people. But some part of his mind knew it was happening here and he was in the middle of it.

Instinctively he turned his face sharply away from the heat and glare, as if he'd been slapped.

He noticed remotely through his shock that the crying woman was gone, and he was lying on the floor.

Time gave a lurch, and he heard himself say, "Oh, good Christ! Danny!"

Wondering with a thrust of dread if the plane that exploded was Flight 109 from Phoenix.

2

Nudger sat up and looked around vaguely, as if trying to distinguish dream from reality. A shrill sound was echoing around the inside of his skull: a woman screaming over and over, mindlessly. Then came silence, the trauma of shock washing over the corridor like a wave.

Nudger, perhaps more used to sudden violence than most, cautiously took stock. No one seemed to be seriously hurt. The boy who'd been standing at the window was on his mother's lap now, and she was holding a handkerchief pressed to his arm. Cut by flying glass, probably, when the window was blown in. Nudger saw now that several people were nursing cuts. He looked and felt over his own body, using anxious hands to explore; he seemed to be uninjured.

Outside, the blackened shell of the aircraft was still burning. It was surrounded by emergency equipment and scurrying figures. White foam was being sprayed on it from a yellow-and-chrome pumper. Two men in bright yellow slickers were hosing what appeared to be water onto the tail section, pumped from a fire engine with flashing red-and-blue lights. What looked like three scorched bodies were lying near the plane. As Nudger watched, another man in a yellow slicker methodically spread a blue tarpaulin over one of the bodies. Black smoke hovered above the airport like a low and menacing storm cloud, but the lightning had already struck.

Nudger stood up, swayed, then found his balance. Glass crunching beneath his shoes, he made his way over to the monitors displaying arriving flights. Because of delays, half a dozen flights other than Danny's were due in at approximately the time of the explosion. A man standing next to Nudger was staring in quiet horror at the monitors, suffering the same apprehension as Nudger. Fate had done something terrible; no one knew yet quite what. The TWA ticket agents had disappeared, probably to aid in rescue efforts. Within a few minutes several dozen people were standing beneath the monitors, gazing up at them like supplicants seeking mercy from a deity. No one made a sound other than ragged breathing.

Finally, the arrival time after Flight 243 from New York to St. Louis, flickered away and was replaced by SEE AGENT. The great god Microchip had spoken. Several people groaned. A woman fainted and a knot of people gathered around her.

Nudger heard his own breath trail from his lungs. Relief was tainted by his compassion for the woman on the floor, moaning now that she'd lost her husband. "Charles! . . ."

A voice said, "Nudge, what happened?"

Nudger turned. Danny was standing there with his black garment bag slung over his shoulder, basset-hound features more somber than usual, sad dark eyes bewildered. Nudger gave him a hug and pumped his hand. Danny backed away a few steps and looked even more confused. Something was going on, but he wasn't sure what. Danny was used to that.

"The plane from New York blew up," Nudger said.

Danny didn't seem to comprehend this. He said, "They let us out at Gate Thirty-five instead of this one. Told us there was some kinda emergency in the airport and hustled us outa the plane. I figured you'd be waiting down here for me." He turned his head and gazed out at the smoking turmoil beyond the glassless windows, understanding at last. "Jesus! Blew up, huh? A bomb?"

"Maybe," Nudger said. He'd dropped Danny off at the airport two days ago and knew the garment bag was his only luggage. "Let's get outa here. I'm parked on the orange level."

When they'd finally located the car on yellow, Nudger paid his way out of the parking garage and took Interstate 70 east, then the Inner Belt south. Wailing emergency vehicles passed them, speeding in the opposite direction. He switched the old Granada's air conditioner to High but it didn't help much; needed a charge of Freon, the guy at the service station had told Nudger. Nudger would take care of that as soon as his bank account got a charge of currency. Money, the glue and grease of society.

"Hot out in Phoenix, too," Danny said, staring out at the sunstruck oncoming traffic flashing past on the other side of the median rail. He still didn't seem to grasp the significance of what had occured.

"I'll bet." Nudger saw again the brilliant orange blast and the silhouettes of the mother and her two kids etched against the glowing window overlooking the runways. Heard the brittle music of the glass caving in.

"You think terrorists blew up that plane, Nudge?"

"Too early to know. The FAA will examine the wreckage. Then the FBI will investigate."

"Doesn't look like they'll be able to tell much from what's left," Danny said. "Nothing there but a lotta burned metal and stuff."

"You'd be surprised. They can tell if it was a bomb. Maybe even what kinda bomb it was."

"You think it was a bomb?"

"I'm not sure," Nudger said. "I saw where the explosion started. Above where the left wing joined the plane's body. A bomb, though, I dunno. It'd be speculation. Have to know about airplanes to figure a bomb for sure."

"Terrorists or whatever, the guys that blow up planes, don't get caught very often, do they?"

"Doesn't seem so," Nudger said, exiting the highway at Eager Road. His stomach was pulsating.

He waited parked in the shade, perspiring and listening to blues on KDHX, while Danny left the garment bag in his apartment and changed clothes. Then they drove east on Manchester to the doughnut shop and Nudger's office. Nudger parked by the broken meter on the other side of the street. That would make up some for being overcharged for parking at the airport. Balance, justice, was important in the world, and lacking.

"Think you shoulda hung around the airport, Nudge?" Danny asked. "Told what you saw?"

"Me and a couple hundred people probably saw the same thing," Nudger said. He slammed the car door. Didn't bother locking it. He'd managed to pay his insurance this time around.

They stood in the heat and waited for a break in traffic on Manchester, then jogged across the street, sucking in exhaust fumes. Nudger could feel the excess fat around his middle jouncing with each step. He was far from being fat, but there was no denying he'd developed a slight stomach paunch the past year or so. *Old bastard in his mid-forties; gotta get in shape.*

Danny jingled a big ring of keys and let himself into the doughnut shop to get set up for tomorrow, when he'd reopen with fresh hits for cholesterol addicts.

Nudger opened the door off to the side and trudged up the narrow stairwell to his office door, listening to the old wooden stairs creak. He liked the fact that the steps made noise; it announced visitors. Now and then they were clients, and Nudger had a chance to straighten his tie or get his feet off the desk before they came in, maybe pull some paper or a file folder in front of him and look industrious. There was only one chance to make a good first impression.

The office air was stale and hot. As soon as he entered he crossed to the window and turned on the air conditioner. It hummed, gurgled, clinked and promised to do its best, but July in St. Louis was a challenge, usually a losing battle.

He looked at the morning mail that he'd scooped up from

the landing: a couple of bills, and a letter from his former wife, Eileen, no doubt demanding back alimony and threatening legal action. He wished he could pay her and get her off his back, but he barely made enough to survive, while she was earning a fortune in one of those home products pyramid sales companies. She was regional manager now, which meant she got a percentage of the earnings of every salesperson in her area. It also meant she had more free time to harass Nudger.

He didn't open any of the envelopes. Tossed them on a corner of the desk with some other unread mail.

In one motion, he slumped in his squealing swivel chair behind the desk and punched Play on his answering machine.

Beep! "This is Eileen, Nudger. If you know what's—"

Good God! He pressed Fast Forward.

Beep! "I don't talk to machines. Have your machine call my machine and they can talk about the business you lost."

Beep! "If you want to hear about a truly revolutionary breakthrough group life insurance plan for the self-employed call me, Jerry, at—"

Enough! Nudger wasn't interested in group life insurance. What were the odds of being killed in a group? Anyway, who would he name as beneficiary? Eileen? He shuddered. He didn't like the idea of being worth more to her dead than alive. Her lawyer might be able to get him executed.

He spent the rest of the afternoon at his secondhand IBM Selectric, typing reminders to people who owed him money. Once he thought he heard a creak on the stairs. Maybe a client. But nobody came through the door. Probably it had been the wind. A summer shower was blowing in from the west. Now and then a drop of rain pinged off the metal air conditioner.

Within half an hour it was thundering and raining hard. Which did nothing positive for Nudger's mood. He switched on the yellow-shaded desk lamp. That helped some, but the office was still gloomy, and the yellow-hued flesh on his hands and bare forearms suggested he had jaundice. As soon as the rain let up, he grabbed his ragged black umbrella and got out of there.

That night, in his apartment on Sutton, he microwaved a frozen turkey dinner and ate it with a helping of two-day-old salad he'd brought home in a doggy bag from a restaurant. Then he settled down on the sofa in front of the TV to watch one of the local news teams and sat patiently through the introductory bad comedy.

Guess what was the lead story. One of the talking hairdos was describing the airline tragedy, while behind him a tape of the burning plane and hopeless rescue efforts was shown over and over. Ninety-three people had been killed when an explosion near the wing tanks ignited jet fuel. Some of the survivors were on the critical list. When another local hairdo kept shoving a microphone into the face of a weeping relative of one of the victims, Nudger squeezed the remote and switched to national news on Channel 9, the MacNeil Lehrer Report.

There, too, the subject was the destroyed plane. MacNeil was interviewing a representative of the Federal Aviation Administration, an FBI agent, and an expert on terrorism. The FAA man, a calm and neutral sort with gray hair and a gray suit, said the death toll would most likely climb higher. The FBI guy, obsessed with explanations, said the plane's passenger list was being checked out, along with security measures at Kennedy in New York, the airport where the doomed flight had originated.

"Aren't bombs usually set with timers or barometric devices to explode when the airliner is at high altitude?" soberfaced MacNeil asked.

"Indeed," said the terrorist expert, who himself had anarchist's eyes. "Perhaps this one malfunctioned."

"We'll probably discover a great deal more about the bomb," the FBI guy said. "Witnesses saw in which part of the plane it was detonated, and investigators at the scene have already recovered parts of it that survived the explosion."

Nudger felt his stomach twitch. He'd heard more than enough about the airline disaster. It was a sore area his mind recoiled from. Like avoiding remembering a nightmare. Christ, ninety-three people!

"You're all agreed, then," MacNeil said, "that it was a bomb that destroyed the plane?"

"It was a bomb," said the man from the FAA.

"It was a bomb," said the FBI guy.

The terrorist expert said, "There's no doubt the plane was blown up by a bomb."

"Has any terrorist group—"

Just as Nudger pressed Mute, the phone jangled. He considered ignoring it, but it was persistent. On the fifth ring, he reached over and dragged it toward him by the cord. *Clatter, clatter, ding, ding.* He lifted the receiver.

Danny was on the other end of the connection. He said, "Hear the news about that plane, Nudge? They say it was a bomb."

3

The next morning, Nudger stopped at the Hardee's on Manchester before driving to the office. He used the coupon from yesterday's *Post-Dispatch* to get a bacon-and-egg biscuit for only seventy-nine cents, then carried that and a cup of coffee to a booth and settled in to gaze out the window at rush hour traffic while he ate.

There was something mesmerizing about watching the stream of cars carrying people on their way to normal occupations. Nine-to-fivers leading largely uneventful and happy enough lives. If he'd been suitable for any other profession after being eased out of the police department because of his nervous stomach, he wouldn't have become a private investigator. He wasn't in it for the money, that was for sure. He knew he could, and should, start from scratch somewhere, learn to sell appliances or used cars, maybe. Eileen and her lawyer would like that. He'd have a salary to attach.

He was surprised when police lieutenant Jack Hammersmith slid his bulk onto the orange bench seat across the table. Hammersmith's protruding stomach was pressing against the table so that a button rested almost horizontally on the wood-look Formica. He put down his tray, on which were four cinnamon rolls, coffee, and orange juice, and said, "I called your apartment but got no answer. Checked down the street at your office and in Danny's, but you weren't there."

"How'd you know I was here?" Nudger asked. The scent of the cinnamon rolls was making him hungry for something sweet and damn the calories. Hammersmith the bad influence.

"Coupons in yesterday's paper. If you weren't eating breakfast on the house at Danny's, I knew where to look. You follow the bargains in biscuits."

Nudger nodded. "I didn't feel like going face-to-face with a Dunker Delite this morning. Even a free one."

"That I understand. You look like hell. Rough time last night?"

"Not much sleep," Nudger said. "I'm having one of those lives. I was out at the airport to meet Danny yesterday. Saw what happened to that airliner. Don't wanna see anything like it again ever."

"You spent time as a cop, Nudge. You oughta be used to that sorta thing."

"Never did get used to it. That's why I'm not still a cop."

Hammersmith was grinning. Nudger had once saved his life, when they were partners in a two-man patrol car, and he'd never forgotten, never stopped being grateful. But he liked to goad Nudger, knew about his nervous stomach and liked to press. Ever since he'd made lieutenant and grown obese, he'd been sadistic.

"You look me up for a reason?" Nudger asked. "Or did you just wanna break bread together?"

"Little of each, Nudge. I thought you oughta know what I heard from somebody over at the Civil Courts Building. Eileen and her lawyer are planning to go after you again in a major way for back alimony. Also get the amount you pay each month increased."

"Nothing new there," Nudger said. He thought about Eileen's lawyer, Henry Mercato. Contemptible little bastard. He and Eileen might be sleeping together, mating like a couple of sharks in dark water.

"Well, the fresh wrinkle is Mercato's got somebody keeping an eye on Claudia. The angle's gonna be you're spending money on Claudia that should go to Eileen."

Nudger's stomach throbbed with anger. This was really too much. He put down his bacon-and-egg biscuit on its crinkled wrapper. "A big date for Claudia and me is a ball game that includes a hot dog. Some of the time she pays."

Hammersmith grinned. "So whoever's following you better like baseball and wieners." He wolfed down a cinnamon roll as if it were a peanut, then dabbed delicately at his lips with his napkin. "I just figured you should know about it, in case you notice some guy hanging around the two of you."

Nudger sipped his coffee. "Thanks, Jack."

"Nothing, Nudge. You say you were there when that airliner went boom?"

"Yeah. I was waiting to drive Danny home from flying out to visit his cousin in Phoenix. Explosion took out the window I was looking through."

"Traumatic for you, I guess." There went another cinnamon roll. Two bites this time. As he chewed, Hammersmith's smooth-shaven jowls waggled where they spilled over his blue shirt collar. Each year it got more difficult to remember the young, slim and handsome Hammersmith who'd ridden a patrol car and charmed and cajoled even the hardest addicts and prostitutes. "Least they got the bastard."

"Huh?"

"You haven't read the paper this morning?"

"No. I got outa bed and came straight here. Didn't even listen to the car radio."

"New York police were called when a suicide was discovered with his wrists slit in a New York hotel room. Checked in under a phony name. Smith, if you can believe it. No identification until they found a travel agency receipt in the room. He was booked on the flight that blew up. No ticket in the room, though. Airline records show he boarded, so he probably used the half-guilty passenger scam."

"Half-guilty passenger?"

"Yeah. That's when some innocent person's led to think they're carrying something illegal. Maybe liquor no duty's been paid on. Maybe a small amount of drugs. Whoever bought the ticket pays them plenty to lug a suitcase or briefcase on a flight, and they don't know they're really carrying a bomb. None of them ever complain about being tricked, though. How terrorists work."

"And everyone would think the guy who bought the ticket boarded the plane and was dead."

"For a while, anyway. Until he had a chance to get outa the country to wherever international law would protect him."

"Was this dead guy in New York a terrorist?"

"Doesn't seem that way so far, but you know how it goes. Investigation of that kinda thing takes time. Anyway, the crash-site experts know the bomb went off under or near the seat he had reserved."

"And where somebody was sitting in his place, having used his ticket."

"Uh-huh. And there's no way to identify what's left of whoever was occupying the seat when the bomb exploded. The blast was too destructive." The last two rolls were promptly devoured, along with the orange juice. Hammersmith sipped at the coffee then frowned and said, "How piss must taste."

"Bottom of the pot, maybe."

"I figured you were in here, so the sludge at the bottom must already be in your cup. Your fate, sorta, to get the bottom of the pot."

Nudger couldn't disagree.

Hammersmith's bloated pink hands gathered foam cups and wadded paper napkins so they wouldn't fall off his tray. Then he worked his bulk out of the booth and stood up. "See ya, Nudge. I gotta go fight crime. Enjoy the rest of your bargain breakfast."

Nudger watched him walk from the restaurant and cross the blacktop parking lot. Hammersmith moved with extraordinary grace for such a fat man. Glided like a ballroom dancer. He wedged himself behind the wheel of his unmarked Ford, started the engine, and drove from the lot to turn east on Manchester, heading for the Third District station and the war on crime.

Nudger got up and walked over to where some newspapers supplied by the restaurant were jutting from a wooden rack on the wall. He thumbed through them until he found a front-page section and carried it back to the booth. Sipping his coffee, he read about the airliner bomber.

It was as Hammersmith had said. The dead man's real name was Rupert Winslow. He'd been thirty-nine years old when he'd bled to death in the bathtub of his room at the Meridian Hotel in New York. No suicide note was found in the room. Authorities said that Winslow at this point didn't seem to be affiliated with any terrorist group.

Nudger shoved the paper aside. It was hard to imagine a man named Rupert Winslow being mixed up with Middle East terrorism; he should be using his time playing croquet or riding to hounds. But it could happen. Maybe the IRA was responsible, though blowing up airplanes, especially in the United States, didn't seem to fit their style or motive. Nudger figured the authorities would discover Winslow had some kind of mental trouble in his past. Or maybe the bombing was the result of ice-cold calculation, an insurance murder, and he'd had second thoughts and a load of guilt that prompted him to commit suicide. Whatever. It wasn't Nudger's problem.

Until he drove to his office and found the crying woman from the airport seated in the chair alongside his desk. She hadn't switched on the air conditioner and was perspiring in the early heat.

She wasn't crying now.

She looked scared.

4

She stood up when Nudger entered. Started to say something then changed her mind and clamped her lips together. She was, as he'd thought at the airport, an attractive woman when not weeping. Whipped cream complexion. An oval face with generous features. Pointed chin. Pouty lower lip that suggested volcanic passion. Blue eyes that were perhaps set too close together and gave her a rather intent expression. Or maybe it was fear lending her that look.

She was wearing navy blue slacks and a silky gray blouse today. A silver neck chain that played with the light. Blue high-heeled shoes with leather buckles on the insteps. Expensive clothes. Stylish.

Nudger decided he'd better ooze some charm her way, gave her the old sweet smile and said, "Sit back down, please." He walked over and switched on the air conditioner. *Click! Hmmm. Gurgle.* "You shoulda done this," he said. Cooling air stirred the hair on his arm. "No reason you had to sit there and bake."

Back in the chair, she tried a smile but it wavered and

dissolved. "Not my office. Besides, I was told by the man downstairs in the doughnut shop you'd be here any minute." She was clutching something white—the business card he'd handed her yesterday at the airport. She saw him staring at it. "When I left after the explosion, I just picked this up from where I'd laid it. I don't know why. But I think maybe it must mean something, that I did that."

Nudger sat down behind his desk and watched the woman wince as his swivel chair squealed. He smiled again, swiveled without realizing it. *Eeek!* "You know *my* name."

The woman realized what he meant and said, "Oh, I'm Vanita Lane. When I got home yesterday, I saw what kinda card this was. I mean, your profession."

Nudger liked that. Not many people called what he did a profession. "And you decided you need my services?"

"Yes."

"You're frightened."

"It shows?"

"Sure does. Unless somebody snuck in here and converted that to a vibrating chair."

She glanced down and saw how her hands were trembling. She folded them tightly in her lap, pale against the blue material, and tried to hold them still. Muscle ridged beneath the creamy flesh of her arms.

Nudger said, "Yesterday at the airport you were crying."

"I would be today," she told him, "only there's a limit to how much a person can cry. And now, as you pointed out, I'm scared."

"Why? Why were you at the airport yesterday?"

"Two questions."

"Yep. Calls for two answers."

She bowed her head, as if praying for the rare combination of strength and wisdom, then raised it and locked her apprehensive blue gaze on him. So intense. "I wanted to know if that plane would land okay."

"You suspected it might be blown up?"

She nodded.

Nudger's stomach, as usual a beat ahead of his brain, did a couple of flips. Whoa! Federal crime. Ninety-three victims. This was getting heavy. Maybe dangerous.

He said, "So why didn't you notify the airline? Try to stop what happened?"

"I couldn't. And there was a good chance it *wouldn't* happen. God, if I'd known for sure . . ."

"You'd have phoned TWA?"

She gnawed on her nifty lower lip and looked past Nudger out the window. He heard a pigeon flapping around and cooing on the ledge. Christ, he hated pigeons! "I think so," she said, "but who knows? I've gotta be honest, or there'd be no sense to my coming here. There was still something between me and Ropes."

"Ropes?"

"Rupert Winslow."

"The Rupert Winslow found dead with his wrists slit in New York?"

"Yeah. The people who knew him called him Ropes. A nickname because . . . well, he had that reputation. Knew the ropes."

"Not all of them," Nudger said.

"Guess not."

"The authorities think he tricked someone into carrying the bomb on board the airliner."

"He did. In a way. But he didn't really intend to kill all those people. He had to be more horrified over what happened than anyone."

Nudger didn't quite buy that; most of the dead passengers had families. "Is that why he committed suicide? Guilt? Grief?"

Vanita sighed. Swallowed. Suddenly her hands were still. "No way was it suicide. Ropes was murdered."

Zoom went Nudger's stomach, up into his throat where his heart moved over to make room. *Murder* was perhaps the word he liked least.

She said, "This is really about diamonds." As if somehow

that negated what had happened to Flight 243 and might put his mind at ease. Heck, diamonds had caused little enough trouble in this world.

"Jewelry or baseball?" Nudger asked. Always he tried to be cute when he was scared. Even he understood it was a defense mechanism, but he couldn't control his reaction.

"Neither. Unmounted diamonds. Over a million dollars' worth. They were stolen from a diamond merchant in New York. Ropes helped set up the deal, for a commission. And everything went as planned. But afterward he got adventuresome and tried to steal the diamonds from the thieves. They found out and got them back. That's when he phoned me from his hotel in New York. Ropes always came to me when there was trouble."

"You were lovers?"

"For a while. But even after things cooled off between us he still sort of depended on me. We stayed more than friends, less than lovers. This'll sound silly, but Ropes never knew his mother, and I'm a few years older than him—than he was."

"Older and wiser?"

She gave him that intense look. "In some ways."

"So he phoned from New York and told you about this diamond thing," Nudger said, prodding her to continue.

"And he told me the precaution he had taken in case the original thieves discovered who'd stolen the diamonds from them and came to get them back. He had them in an attaché case, in with some bath salts, so you'd have to pour out the contents of the bottle to see which crystals were diamonds. The other stuff in the case was what lots of overnight business travelers would carry. Some computer printouts, a fresh shirt, shaving kit, that sorta thing. Even some dirty underwear to discourage anybody from looking real close. But Ropes learned about demolition in the army. And the attaché case itself was lined with Semtex."

"Semtex?"

"It's a powerful plastic explosive. The attaché case was actually a bomb. The detonator was in the lead-lined handle so it'd pass undetected through airport X-ray equipment."

A weakness swept over Nudger. *Ninety-three people.* Why hadn't airport security been more alert? His voice quavered. "Where was the timing device?"

"That's just it, there was none. The attaché case was set up to explode the second time the lid was opened and closed. That way whoever stole the diamonds would check on them, put them back in the case, and take the case to wherever they were going. Where the next time they opened and closed it they'd be killed. At least that was how Ropes had it figured."

"Obviously his figuring was wrong."

"Tragically wrong. He told me that two of the men who'd stolen the diamonds from the merchant came to his hotel and made him reveal where they were. Threatened him with a knife until he talked. Then they'd taken the diamonds and the case, along with his airline ticket, and left. They knew he couldn't go to the police, so there was plenty of time for them to do what they wanted with him if they had revenge in mind. They told him that before they left. Said they wanted him to think about it."

Nudger nodded, understanding. "So you knew someone was on the plane in Rupert Winslow's seat, carrying a briefcase that couldn't be opened and closed one more time without an explosion."

She worked her jaw muscles, then said, "That's right. So I wanted to come to the airport to . . . make sure the plane got down all right."

"But it didn't."

"No. Probably the man with the attaché case wanted to check its contents one more time before getting off the plane."

"And when the surviving diamond thieves heard on the news about the bomb going off, they realized they'd lost the diamonds. So they went back to the Meridian Hotel and took it out on Winslow."

Vanita's voice was soft. He had to strain to hear it. "That

must have been how it was. They made it look like he'd killed himself. And in a way he did, when he stole the diamonds. He always pushed his luck, Ropes did. This time he pushed it over the edge."

Nudger looked out the window. The pigeon on the ledge looked in at him and cocked its head.

"Mr. Nudger?"

"You have to go to the FBI," he said. "Tell them what you told me."

"Like I said, I can't. I knew about the diamond theft, so I'm an accessory. Knew about what was in the attaché case, so I'm an accessory to that crime, too. Even though I was sitting in the airport crying and praying it wouldn't happen."

"I've gotta give this information to the authorities," Nudger said. "Professional obligation. You must have realized that before you came here."

"I came here because I thought when you heard me out you'd decide not to pass on what I told you. For a number of reasons."

Nudger said, "Start ticking them off." What the hell, give the woman her say.

"First of all, the airliner bombing's been solved by the authorities. Ropes really *is* guilty. Legally, anyway. And the identity of the passenger who traveled in his place will probably never be learned. So the plane getting blown up is closed business."

"What about the diamond theft? I'm supposed to report a felony to the police. Might have to find some other line of work if I don't."

"I don't know anything about the original theft. Only that it took place and there were several men involved. Honest, that's all Ropes told me."

Nudger leaned back in his chair. *Sqeeeeeeek!* He thought about that.

"Also," Vanita said, "if you tell anyone about this conversation I'll deny it took place. You can't prove I told you any of this, you know."

Point.

"Then there's this," she said. She reached into the black purse resting against a chair leg and drew out a thick white business envelope, unsealed. She tossed it onto Nudger's desk. The crisp green corners of folding money peeked out the top. "A thousand dollars, Mr. Nudger. Your retainer."

"For doing what?"

"This morning my phone rang. When I picked it up nobody talked to me. All I heard was this wheezy kinda breathing."

"Kinky sex?"

"I doubt it. The breathing was more like somebody was sick. Somebody who called just to check and see if I was home. I got scared, then I got out of the house. Remembered you and found your card in my purse. I need your help, Mr. Nudger."

It took Nudger only a few seconds to see what she was driving at. He didn't blame her for being skittish. "Listen, don't play around with this. You need to go to the police. Tell them what you told me."

"I will, but only if what I want you to do doesn't work."

"That's a crazy way to look at your situation."

"Maybe. But if it gets too dangerous I'll do as you say and go to the cops. I promise."

Don't listen, Nudger told himself. Hold your ears.

But he did listen, all the time staring at the envelope on his desk. Thinking about Eileen and Henry Mercato, who at that moment were possibly working out legal strategy against him. And here in this envelope was the solution to his problems— at least for a while.

Vanita said, "The people who stole the diamonds might think I have them. Or that Ropes mailed them to me and I've got them or I'm about to receive them."

"How would they even know about you? Know about the phone call?"

"I'm not sure. Ropes called me from a public phone, not the one in his room. So the hotel would have no record. But he carried my photograph, along with my phone number, in his wallet. It's, uh, the kind of photo that leaves little doubt about our relationship. At least the kind of relationship we used to have. And the news account of his death said his wallet was missing. My guess is whoever used the plane ticket took it, just in case identification was needed that matched the name on the ticket."

"Ah!" Nudger said, wondering about the photo. It had no doubt been destroyed in the explosion, along with the wallet and whoever was carrying it.

"I want you to protect me," Vanita said. "But just as important, I need you at some point to convince whoever's after me that I don't have the diamonds."

"At which time you'll no longer need protection."

"Exactly."

Nudger said, "Do you?"

"Do I what?"

"Have the diamonds."

"No. I'm telling you the truth."

"I thought you said the thieves knew the diamonds were in the attaché case. They left the hotel room with them."

"That's what Ropes told me. But the friends of the man who died on the plane might think they were paste. Might not think Ropes would deliberately blow up the loot. Maybe the plan was for all of them to be somewhere when the bomb went off, and that would leave only Ropes still alive and with the diamonds. It was just the sorta thing Ropes might have planned."

A thousand dollars.

"Mr. Nudger? Am I your client?"

Nudger said, "This sounds dangerous." He was trying to talk himself out of it. She wanted him to push his luck, the way Rupert Winslow had pushed his, over the edge.

"But you'll do it?"

He looked out the window again. The pigeon was still there, puffing out its chest and staring insolently at him as if he, Nudger, had no right to be in the office. No right to be in the world. Couldn't even fly. The blissful confidence of stupidity, all wrapped up in feathers.

"I'll do it," he said, still looking at the pigeon.

He heard Vanita sigh in relief. "I'm glad you want to help me. Even if it's for the money."

"It's not just the money," Nudger said. "I've got this thing about tilting at windmills."

But he wondered, was it only the money? Old root of all evil?

He thought he could afford to play the job a little light and not be totally terrified. Because Vanita was wrong about one thing: If the diamonds were on that plane, FAA investigators would find some if not all of them. It would take more than an explosion to destroy diamonds, which were even harder than Eileen's heart. And every inch of ground would be scrutinized at the crash site.

As soon as news of the diamonds got out, whoever was after Vanita would realize she didn't have them and back away from her. That would be that. And Nudger would have earned his thousand dollars. Well, not earned actually . . .

That was how he had it worked out, anyway. He thought he had a handle on the situation.

He and the pigeon.

5

"Got any relatives here in the city?" Nudger asked. "Anyplace you could go and stay outa sight for a while?"

"I only have one living relative," Vanita said. "Marlou. Only I don't wanna get her involved in this in any way. She's not like I am and doesn't deserve this kind of trouble, even secondhand."

"Marlou?"

"My baby sister. Her name's really Marcy Lou Dee. Dee's my maiden name. Lane's the name of my ex-husband. He died seven years ago in a car accident."

"Marcy Lou Dee," Nudger repeated. He thought it sounded like a Woolworth's perfume.

"Everybody's called her Marlou since she was young," Vanita said.

He studied her. "What do you mean when you say your sister's not like you?"

She smiled slightly and looked off to the left, the way psychologists say right-handed people do when they're searching their memories. Nudger had never put much stock in that one. "We're only a few years apart, and we grew up down in southwest Missouri near the Arkansas line."

"The Ozarks," Nudger said.

"Very much so. Anyway, I got outa there soon as I could. Went off to state college in Cape Girardeau. Truth is, I was kinda ashamed of my hillbilly origins. Marlou never was. Still isn't. Country girl and proud of it, and there's nothing wrong with that, I guess. Only, sorry, it's just not the way I was built. She didn't leave home till our parents died and there was nothing there for her. Then she came to the city four years ago and I helped her get a job. We still see each other at least once a month."

"Marlou know Rupert Winslow?"

"She met Ropes a few times, that's all. We lead different lives. I told you, we're nothing alike. She's two-step and I'm fox-trot."

Could be the next Barry Manilow hit. "Anyplace you'd be missed if you danced out of sight for a week or two?"

"I arrange loans for an investment company. There won't be any questions asked if I call and tell them I'm taking a few weeks off."

Nudger stood up, rapped on the window behind the desk, and watched with satisfaction as the startled pigeon flapped away. He noticed it had defecated messily on the window ledge. They always did that. He smiled at Vanita, showing her he had everything under control, knew exactly what to do. "You drive here?"

She nodded, staring up at him with those blue, blue eyes. Why was he such a sucker for blue eyes? Claudia's eyes were brown. So he was a sucker for brown eyes sometimes, too. He said, "I'll follow you back to your place, then you can pack some things and we'll get you checked into a motel."

She looked uneasy, as if she might be considering arguing. It was no fun staying cooped up in a motel room for an indefinite period, especially for a woman like this—fox-trotter and lover of the late Ropes Winslow. But she said, "Sounds like the smart thing to do," and stood up and smoothed her slacks over her shapely thighs.

She bent over and lifted her purse from the floor, smiled at him and said, "Well, let's go."

Nudger followed her late-model blue BMW west on Manchester out to Lindbergh, then north. She turned onto St. Charles Rock Road, drove a short distance, and made a right turn. Almost immediately she made a hard left onto a side street that led to a modern apartment project. It was a sprawling, two-story complex of beige brick buildings with flat roofs and black wrought-iron balconies. Sunlight sparked blue off a swimming pool visible between two of the buildings. Nudger heard the resonant sprong of a diving board, a faint splash.

Vanita had a second-floor unit in the first building. Spacious and airy, with wall-to-wall green carpeting, glass-topped tables, a low-slung leather sofa, and chrome-framed modern prints on the walls. Place looked as if she'd hired a decorator to choose color and texture and match this with that. Or maybe she'd bought the furnished display unit when the project sold out. It had that feel about it; a place where strangers walked through and were afraid to touch anything.

"Nice apartment," hypocrite Nudger said, as she bustled down the hall toward a back bedroom.

"Used to be a display unit," she called back. "I bought it completely furnished."

He sat down on the sofa, clasped his hands behind his head, and smiled. You're some detective, he told himself.

He heard Vanita moving around in the bedroom for a while. Sliding closet doors rumbled on their rollers. Dresser drawers growled open and shut. Something soft but heavy went *thump*!

After about ten minutes she labored back into the living room dragging a gigantic red suitcase and carrying a long matching garment bag stuffed with so many clothes it was almost round.

"Got everything you need?" he asked.

"I think so." She'd missed the irony.

"You probably won't be coming back here till this is settled," he told her.

"Yeah, I understand that. You don't mind, I wanna drop by my bank. Pick up some cash to take with me."

"Good idea," Nudger said. He was glad the thousand dollars she'd given him hadn't cleaned out her account. Apparently she made good money arranging financing. Might be richer than Eileen. Nudger didn't feel so bad now about accepting the generous cash retainer.

Like a pre-Friedan gentleman he relieved her of the burden of the luggage. It was even heavier than it looked. Vanita didn't say anything when he grunted with effort as he hoisted the suitcase.

She locked the apartment door carefully, then led the way down the stairs to the vestibule. The suitcase, and the bag slung over Nudger's shoulder, bumped banister and wall. Taut nylon scraping over plaster made a sound that set his teeth on edge as if he'd been sucking lemons.

After he'd fitted the luggage into her car's trunk, he got in the Granada and followed her to a savings and loan in Northwest Plaza shopping center. He went inside with her to breathe a little air-conditioned oxygen. Few places were cooler than institutions that handled large sums of money. It wasn't called cold cash for nothing.

He watched her make her transaction at the counter, then they went back outside into heat that felt all the more fierce and drove from the parking lot. This time he led the way in the Granada.

They drove south on Lindbergh, then east on Watson Road. By the time the Granada led the BMW into the parking lot of the Dropp Inn Motel, Nudger was sweating heavily. His shirt was plastered to his shoulder blades. The temperature was skyrocketing outside, and the Granada's air conditioner still thought it was a furnace.

The Dropp Inn was a holdover from the time Watson Road had been old Route 66. It was made up of individual, peak-roofed cottages larger than ordinary motel rooms. Architectural style was of the Hansel and Gretel school. The place was run-down but clean, and Vanita would have some space as well as privacy. The roof of each cottage was topped with an aluminum crosslike TV antenna, though a sign above the office had bragged of cable TV with Home Box Office.

As they stood inside the door of Cottage 13 and looked around at mismatched furniture, dime store still-life prints, the old blond television set, and the antique iron bed, Vanita said, "I'd have chosen a place with more class."

"That's why you're here," Nudger told her. "Let whoever might be looking for you roam around the downtown Hilton."

He was familiar with the cottages and knew there was no back door. While Vanita was testing the air conditioner, he checked the windows and saw that they were locked. Even the tiny frosted glass one in the gray-tiled bathroom was secure.

Vanita was standing next to the humming air conditioner, nodding with satisfaction. "I'll be cool, anyway."

"And well fed. There are some fast-food restaurants within easy walking distance."

"You mean you don't want me to live like a hermit?"

"I don't think you could. Not for very long. And the odds of whoever might be looking for you running across you at Wendy's munching a hamburger are slim."

"Slimmer than I'll be after a week or two of hamburgers."

Nudger grinned. "They serve salads, too." He walked to the door. "Phone my office every morning and evening. Leave a message if I'm not there. I wanna know you're all right while I nose around. And before I go, I need the key to your apart-ment."

"How come?"

"If anyone does want to find you and talk about the dia-monds, that's where they'll start to look."

She seemed to consider that for a moment, then said, "Makes sense." She reached into her purse for her key ring, then detached a brass door key and handed it to him. "It fits the front and back doors."

The key was warm from her hand. He slipped it into his pocket. "You read?"

"Read?"

"Yeah. You know." He pointed to his eyes. Mimed turning a page.

"Sure, I told you I went to college." Ah! A little sarcasm. He hoped.

"I mean for pleasure. Books, magazines."

"No, not much. Financial statements are what I mostly read. *Cosmopolitan* now and then."

Nudger wasn't surprised. "I'll drop by tomorrow and bring you the latest issue."

"Okay, thanks." She glanced around. "I'll be fine here. I'll watch television. The soaps. 'Geraldo.' 'Oprah.' I'll wait to hear what you find out." She sat down on the edge of the bed, making the old springs squeal, and worked her shoes off her feet. Wriggled her toes, whose nails were enameled red to match her fingernails. "This was a good idea, Nudger. I think I can relax here and not be afraid."

"Stay afraid enough not to go out too often," he told her.

"I'll try."

He smiled, reassuringly, he hoped. Then he left her and stood outside the door, listening as she clicked the deadbolt and rattled the chain lock into place.

Good girl. He'd try to remember that *Cosmo*. Maybe pick her up a *TV Guide*.

What the hell, he'd give her his Wendy's coupons.

6

Conscience.

Hammersmith often said Nudger had too much of it, and maybe Hammersmith was right. A thousand dollars was locked in the bottom drawer of Nudger's office file cabinet, and he suspected his services weren't really necessary—or wouldn't be within a few days, as soon as news of the diamonds at the air disaster scene was made public. Then Nudger's client, and her pursuers, would know the game was over. But until then, while there *was* danger to her and to him, Nudger felt compelled to do something to earn his fee.

Dumb, but there it was. Like an affliction.

Conscience.

As he drove north on Lindbergh toward Vanita's apartment, he wondered how much of the thousand dollars he should throw to Eileen to keep her and her lawyer at bay. In this age when few childless, self-supporting women were awarded alimony, Henry Mercato and Eileen had managed to financially rape Nudger. Now Eileen was earning more than twice his annual income, and he was reasonably sure she'd be living openly with Mercato if the intimate domestic arrangement wouldn't upset their plans to wring every dollar possible out of Nudger.

Sated or not, Eileen couldn't stay away from the trough. She didn't operate out of economic necessity; she was motivated by a nasty combination of vengeance and greed, using Mercato the way she'd used Nudger, but Mercato didn't know it. Well, bright and eager as he was, he'd find out eventually. Nudger didn't feel sorry for him. And he didn't want to pay Eileen any more than the court had decided five years ago. Eileen wouldn't be satisfied with that amount, and wouldn't let Mercato be satisfied. Greed and spite would be the thing that slept with them.

Nudger was chomping an antacid tablet by the time he parked in the lot of Vanita's apartment building. It was pointless to dwell on the unchangeable and unpleasant, he told himself. He should be concentrating on what he was doing here, and why. What he'd say and do if someone actually came to Vanita's apartment looking for her and the diamonds.

His stomach growled and suggested something that sounded like "Ruuuuun!" He got out his roll of antacid tablets, thumbed back the silver foil, and popped two more of the chalky white disks into his mouth.

The apartment was stuffy and silent. It was a stupid idea to come here, he told himself, sitting down on the uncomfortable sofa. Its leather upholstery was sticky, like furless flesh still on the cow. Down around the udder. Yuk! He got up and instead sat in some kind of modern canvas sling chair with an angular stainless steel frame. He was astounded to find it comfortable; like discovering Andy Warhol was just plain folks.

So here he was, acting out the work ethic.

He sat in the sling chair for a long time, idly wondering why he wasn't selling used cars or insurance. Then he switched on Vanita's multi-million-dollar stereo setup and misused it by listening to the Cardinals' afternoon game with the Mets.

He got up only a couple of times to peer out the window when he heard a car door slam. Helped himself to a can or two of Busch beer from the refrigerator.

The game was a pitchers' duel that went into extra innings. When Todd Worrell came in and struck out Strawberry to stifle a potential Mets' rally in the thirteenth inning and give the Cards a two-to-one win, Nudger decided to call it a day. Like the Cardinals.

He'd at least put forth an effort; laid his ass on the line for his client. Anything *might* have happened here.

Before leaving he snooped around Vanita's apartment. She wouldn't approve, but there was still danger for Nudger; it was possible he'd need an edge.

Vanita seemed to live reasonably well. Though she'd taken more than enough clothes to the motel, her closet was still stocked with plenty of expensive items. Over a dozen business suits with skirts. Probably thirty pairs of shoes, from joggers to high-heeled boots. Little Imelda Marcos.

He poked through the drawers of a dainty walnut secretary desk in the corner of a spare bedroom that had been converted to an office, saw that she had an ominous Visa balance but other than that was pretty well caught up on her bills. No car payment book, so the BMW was most likely paid for, like Nudger's 1979 Ford Granada.

There was another desk in the room, this one ugly but functional, a gray steel office model. It was full of arcane financial information pertaining to Vanita's work. Interest rate lists. Amortization schedules. None of it as exciting as *Cosmo*.

Nudger perched on the edge of the desk and used the phone to call Claudia. She should just now be arriving home from her last class at Stowe, the girls' private high school out in the country, where she was teaching a ninth-grade summer course in remedial English.

She sounded out of breath when she answered the phone. That was okay; Nudger liked listening to her breathe hard.

"Heard the ringing out in the hall," she explained. "Ran up the last flight of steps to reach it in time."

"Knowing it might be me," Nudger said.

She unleashed her stern teacher's tone: "Don't get over-confident. It's unbecoming."

"I'll drive over," Nudger said. "Stop on the way and pick up something for supper."

"Oh? I thought we might eat out."

"Not tonight. It'd be better if we stayed at your place."

"Why?" Different tone altogether. She'd sensed something in his voice. Woman was psychic.

"I'll explain when I get there."

"Okay." She knew enough not to ask superfluous questions. Knew when to push and when to draw back. It was one of the reasons he loved her. Just one.

He said, "Any red wine left in the Gallo bottle?"

"Four or five inches."

Enough. "Good. See you in about an hour."

He hung up the phone and made another quick round of the apartment, to make sure everything was back the way he'd found it.

Then he locked up carefully and went outside to where the Granada was parked in the sun. The rust on the fenders and beneath the doors made the car look as if it were slowly disintegrating in the heat. Maybe it was. Maybe he was.

He rolled down all the windows before sliding in behind the steering wheel and starting the engine.

As he made a left turn out of the parking lot, he felt good about the way the day had gone.

Until something cold shot through his mind. He was sure he'd locked the car when he'd arrived at Vanita's apartment, but it was *unlocked* when he'd returned to it.

Or *had* he locked it? He reconstructed the scene in his mind. Driving onto the blacktop lot, finding a parking slot, switching off the engine and climbing out of the car.

Then what?

His mind's eye saw a Nudger slipping the keys into his pants pocket, leaving the car unlocked. Saw another Nudger squinting across the car to make sure the passenger-side door was locked, then getting out and punching down the driver's-side lock button. Yet another Nudger keying the lock beneath the door handle, *then* dropping the keys into his pocket and walking away.

But which phantom Nudger struck the right chord in his memory? Were *any* of them correct?

By the time he'd parked in front of Claudia's apartment on Wilmington, he'd convinced himself he hadn't actually locked the Granada.

He was smiling as he jogged up the steps to her door at the head of the second-floor hall, wondering why he'd assumed he'd locked the car in the first place, why he'd worried about it. The mind could sure play tricks.

In her understated way, Claudia looked terrific. She had on her blue dress that was severely tailored to her lean body but couldn't straighten her curves, and she still wore a gold necklace and plain gold loop earrings. She didn't have on any shoes, though. Her nylonned toes were scrunched into the throw rug by the door as she stood waiting for Nudger to kiss her.

He touched his lips to her cool forehead. Rattled the white paper bags he was carrying.

She said, "What's that I smell?"

"White Castle burgers. Ten of them. With fries." White Castle was a fast-food franchise that sold curious little inexpensive square hamburgers on square buns. The beef patties had holes in them and they needed onions to hold the entire affair together. Claudia's South Side neighbors referred to White Castle hamburgers as Belly Bombers, but they kept buying and eating them. They were strangely habit forming. Possibly addictive as cocaine.

Claudia smiled. She had a lean face with a perfectly shaped nose that was too long but lent her a look of nobility. Dark eyes that saw deep into things. The longer you looked at Claudia, the more attractive she grew to be; the longer she looked at you, the more downright beautiful she became. A subtle male-female connection was completed and that was that. The way it was with some women. They were sexy in a way subdued but potent. Low-voltage but high-wattage. She nodded toward the familiar white bags and said, "The wine should go well with those. Let's uncap it so it can breathe and we'll eat." Such sarcasm.

She took the bags from Nudger and carried them to the dining room table. He hung back so he could watch the perfect motion of her walk. Then he went into the kitchen and got the jug of Gallo from behind a carton of milk in the refrigerator. Pulled a couple of clean glasses out of the dishwasher. No need for flatware. White Castle burgers and fries were finger food.

When he sat down across from Claudia at the table, she said, "There's ice cream in the freezer for dessert. We'll let cholesterol run riot."

She dealt out the hamburgers in their little cardboard folders while Nudger poured wine into the water tumblers. The dining room was cool; the air conditioner in the window near the table served both it and the adjoining living room. It was an old, large apartment of the sort found in south St. Louis. Hardwood floors, high ceilings, radiator steam heat. Ornate, enamel-caked woodwork. Some cracked plaster here and there. Nudger liked it. The place felt more like home than his own apartment.

Claudia bit into one of the little square hamburgers. She loved the things but wouldn't admit it. Then she sipped her wine, gazing at Nudger over the glass rim. She put down the glass and said, "You implied over the phone there was a reason we were eating in tonight."

He told her about Eileen and Mercato's gathering assault on the amount of his legally assigned alimony payments. About the rumor that they'd hired someone to follow Nudger and establish that he was throwing money away on Claudia that should be going to Eileen.

"That's bullshit," Claudia said. "We don't very often dine at four-star restaurants."

"Never have, in fact."

"And most of what I wear, I bought with my salary."

"Painful but true," Nudger admitted. He uncrated and ate

one of his miniature burgers. Counted. Six for him, the usual four for Claudia. Ten might not be enough. "The good news," he said, "is I went to work on a fresh case today. So I'll be able to pay Eileen most of what I owe her."

"What kind of case?"

"Has to do with that airliner blowing up."

Claudia looked concerned. "You're not into something political, are you, Nudger?"

"Not politics," Nudger said, "diamonds. But not the kind that are forever." He explained everything to Claudia.

She looked worried. "So you're in danger until news of the diamonds comes out. If it does."

"Why wouldn't it?" Nudger asked around a mouthful of greasy and salty french fries.

"You said the diamonds are stolen. Maybe the police will want to keep it secret that they've been recovered."

"Reason?"

"So they know something the thieves don't know. They could use that to their advantage."

Nudger washed the fries down with a swallow of wine. His fingers were grease-coated and the glass almost slipped from his hand. "Television crap. Stuff like that doesn't happen in the real world. Cops'll want all the credit they can get for recovering the diamonds. Maybe somebody'll get promoted. Believe me, there'll be a news conference, a speech, Channel Five close-ups of the diamonds on a black velvet cloth. You'll see."

"Hope it's soon," Claudia said. She finished her last little hamburger, then drained her glass of wine. "Want to save the bags and wrappers?" she asked. "Use them in court as evidence of your frugality?"

Nudger didn't think she was funny. He felt a little cheap, actually. "I don't eat this stuff just because it's all I can afford," he said defensively. "I like fast food, and economy wine usually tastes as good as the expensive stuff."

She smiled at him, with a certain light deep in her eyes. She said, "Me, too. Let's make love before it makes us sick."

*   *   *

Nudger lay on his back with Claudia's head resting on his bare chest. The ceiling fan rotated steadily overhead and the window air conditioner was humming, but the room was still warm and smelled of stale perspiration and recent sex.

Claudia was sleeping. Her breathing was rhythmic and deep and with each inhalation her lean, tanned arm moved slightly where it was flung across Nudger's body. Now and then her eyelash fluttered and tickled his chest. REM sleep, Nudger figured. He wondered what she might be dreaming.

Whatever other problems they had, sex was good. Claudia was still in her thirties, but he was mid-forties. Not many years away from AARP membership. Sometimes he surprised himself.

He'd just about decided he'd never been more comfortable and contented, and was drifting into sleep, when the phone on the bedside table rang.

Claudia jerked awake. Blinked and snatched up the receiver on the second ring, knocking the bent tube of KY jelly to the floor. She said, "Jus'a min't," and handed the receiver to Nudger.

He pressed cool plastic to his ear. "'Lo."

"Nudge? Hammersmith here. Need you to come over to where I am. Soon as you can get here."

Something in Hammersmith's voice alerted Nudger. "Where are you?"

"Crime scene."

"Give me directions, Jack," Nudger said irritably. He didn't feel like playing word games.

"Know where the Dropp Inn Motel is on Watson Road?"

Nudger swallowed hard. "I know."

"Then you don't need directions." Hammersmith abruptly hung up. He had a quirk when it came to phone conversations; he always liked to break the connection first. It made him feel like he was in control.

The sun was finally giving in and sinking, and the room had become dim. Nudger stood up and turned dazedly in a circle, then made his way into the bathroom and took a quick shower.

Back in the bedroom, he located his underwear and socks, yanked them right-side-out, and started pulling on his clothes. He wanted to be at the Dropp Inn Motel as soon as possible.

"Trouble?" Claudia asked.

"Business."

"Trouble," she said. She was nothing if not astute. "Got time to share it?"

"Don't know yet what kind it is." He had a pretty good idea, but he didn't want to think about it until it was confirmed.

Claudia said, "Hammersmith's still with Homicide, isn't he?"

"I think so," Nudger said. "See my shoes anywhere?"

7

Flashing red-and-blue roofbar lights from police cars illuminated the Dropp Inn Motel. Half a dozen patrol cars, and what looked like an unmarked county police cruiser, were parked at odd angles in the meandering gravel drive that connected the cottages. As Nudger braked the Granada to a halt as close as possible to Cottage 13, he couldn't help thinking that anyone committing adultery here tonight must have had a hell of a scare. And Nudger knew *he* was scared, or he wouldn't be reaching so far to find humor to suppress panic.

The motel was in the county, not the city, so St. Louis County police were in charge of dealing with whatever crime had been committed in the cottage. For particularly serious crimes, such as murder, a team of city and county police was formed to conduct the investigation so it wouldn't be hindered by the metropolitan area's crazy-quilt pattern of mini-municipalities with their own police departments. Apparently that was what was going on now. Serious crime. Nudger paused outside the cottage and popped an antacid tablet while a tan-uniformed county cop eyed him suspiciously. The cop turned half toward him, absently touching heel of hand to butt of holstered revolver.

Nudger moved toward the cottage door, gravel crunching beneath his soles.

"Got business in there, sir?" the cop asked. Very polite. Very official. Robot in uniform.

Hammersmith's voice said, "I invited him to the party. Let him pass."

The county cop backed away. He didn't seem deferential, though. Playing his role.

Nudger looked over and saw Hammersmith standing there holding the cottage door open, looking indeed like a genial host ready to usher a guest into a social gathering. Would he smile and urge Nudger to help himself to hors d'oeuvres?

Nope. He remained serious and said nothing as Nudger squeezed past him into the cottage.

God, it was hot inside! And crowded with plainclothes cops milling around and talking in low tones. A short man with dark hair permed to impossible curliness was packing stainless steel instruments into a brown case. Nudger knew he must be the medical examiner, closing up shop for the night. There was a fetid smell riding the air. It made Nudger's large intestine attack his small. He felt faint, might have staggered.

"You okay, Nudge?" Hammersmith asked.

"Yeah, fine." Hah! Nudger had recognized the smell and braced himself for what it must mean.

"She isn't," Hammersmith said, and pointed to the bed.

Nudger overcame the resistance of his eye muscles and made himself look.

The covers were thrown back and the mattress was dark with the spilled blood that had fouled the air. Where it wasn't stained with blood, the body of Vanita Lane was almost white. She was lying on her back, her arms stretched above her head, her wrists bound together with what looked like electrical cord and then laced to the iron headboard. Her feet were free. She was lying spraddle-legged, with her bare soles almost touching. Her crotch was a dark mass of congealed blood. Nudger's gaze lurched again toward her hands; there'd been something about them. But on the trip up, his eyes locked on Vanita's face and he couldn't look away. Shallow blue eyes seemed to stare back at him with a fogged expression of vague and hopeless horror. The kind of abject terror seen on Halloween and tribal masks, so vivid it has to be unreal, yet it touches something deep in us all. Her features were contorted with a suffering she was now beyond.

Merciful. Merciful that she's dead.

With great effort he tore his gaze from her face. Spun his entire body away from her. From what she'd become. He bent over and choked back the bile that rose and burned like acid in his throat.

"We better go outside, Nudge," Hammersmith said.

He felt Hammersmith's hand on his shoulder, guiding him toward the door. Nudger straightened up and walked unsteadily ahead of him.

The outside air seemed sweet and the night felt cool. Nudger took several deep breaths, as if trying to drown on purity. Tilted back his head and stared up at the stars. They stared back at him, light-years away and disinterested. Time and distance. On the nearest star, Vanita was still alive and might not have yet met Rupert Winslow.

"Sorry. Forgot about your weak stomach," Hammersmith said.

The hell he had. Nudger glared at him.

"You gonna ask me who she is?" Hammersmith said. "'Scuse me, who she *was?*"

Nudger said, "I know who she was. Who found her?"

"Her door was left half open and the lights were on, and a couple of arriving guests glanced in on the way to their cottage. Saw what we saw and called the police."

"She been dead long?"

"The M.E. says her remaining body temperature suggests a couple of hours at the outside. Autopsy'll pin it down closer. Doubtful that'll help us, though."

Nudger jammed his hands in his pockets, feeling in control

of his stomach now, but barely. He said, "How'd you know to phone me?"

"What we do these days at a murder scene is punch the Redial button on the phone, Nudge. See who the victim might have talked with last. In this case, the dead woman's last phone call was to your answering machine. Wanna share with us why?"

"She was my client."

"Hardly speaks well for your services."

"Her name was Vanita Lane."

"Yeah, we got that and her address from the ID in her purse. Asked around to see which guests were driving which cars and found out that's her blue BMW parked over there."

Nudger said, "I need to ask you a favor, Jack."

Hammersmith fired up one of his incredibly horrible smelling cigars, his fat cheeks puffing in and out like a bellows. He flicked closed the lid on his lighter. Hefted the lighter in his hand and then slid it into a pocket. "That sho?" he said around the cigar.

"In a manner of speaking," Nudger said, "I concealed knowledge of a crime, but I thought it'd all be public knowledge by now. I thought the diamonds would be found."

Hammersmith raised pale eyebrows. "Diamondsh?"

"Yeah, stolen diamonds that should be in the wreckage of the airliner that blew up at Lambert Field yesterday."

Hammersmith slowly removed the cigar from his mouth. "Christ, Nudge. Federal stuff."

"But the evidence I withheld had nothing to do with the bombing. The FBI hung that one on the right man. Rupert Winslow, the guy who killed himself in New York."

"But you want me to keep your secret nonetheless. That it, Nudge?"

"Yeah. It could be rough for me to stay licensed if you don't. Understand I'm not asking you to lie for me, Jack. Just not to mention something."

Inhale, exhale on the cigar. The ember signaled Hammersmith's distress. "This is a homicide, Nudge."

"About the homicide I'll tell everything I know, and there are no secrets."

Hammersmith puffed and thought. Then he shifted his bulk so his weight was evenly distributed on both legs. "So talk, Nudge. Then we'll see what I can promise."

Nudger told Hammersmith the entire story.

When he was finished, Hammersmith glanced at Cottage 13 and blew a cloud of smoke that looked red in the reflected illumination of patrol car lights. Smoke from hell. So much smoke it seemed to rise and extinguish some of the stars. For once Nudger didn't mind the smell. It replaced the stench of blood, still thick in his nostrils and at the base of his tongue, where it lay like taste.

"You're right, Nudge," Hammersmith said. "You probably got no worry with the feds; the airline bombing case is already more or less wrapped up. Still, you could confirm they pinned it on the right man and supply them with some explanation."

"Not my civic duty."

Hammersmith shrugged. "Maybe not. It's arguable, seeing as the guy's dead and the investigation's more or less closed."

Nudger said, "What could lose me my livelihood is not mentioning the information about the diamond theft."

"True. And Captain Springer'll want your head on a stake."

Hammersmith meant Captain Leo Springer, a conniving career cop who'd stepped on a lot of throats to reach his present rank and was still stepping. Most of the decent cops in the St. Louis department hated and feared Springer. Private investigators, decent or otherwise, loathed him. He didn't like the idea of anyone not under his command solving crimes, or even contributing. Made the police seem stupid, he'd once told Nudger. Better to let the bad guys run free than do that.

Nudger sighed and looked out at the lights of traffic streaming past on Watson Road. He said, "Well, that's where I am, Jack."

There was a break in the traffic. Nudger became aware of crickets screaming in the darkness behind the cottages. Two people in the nearest cottage, a man and a woman, had the curtains pulled aside and were staring out, part of what was going on and not a part of it.

"I won't conceal the truth for you," Hammersmith said. "But what I'll do is tell one small lie."

Nudger turned and looked at him. "I'm not asking you to lie, Jack. To jeopardize your career."

"I won't be jeopardizing anything," Hammersmith said, "unless you turn fink."

"That's not likely."

"What you told me just now, I'll say you phoned an hour ago and told it to me."

Nudger felt hope flare. Then he gave this some thought. "Springer won't believe you."

"I know. That's why I'm gonna do it. Get a little pleasure outa taunting the little bastard."

"Damn it, Jack—"

"Don't argue, Nudge. And don't worry about me. I don't do this kinda shit unless I know it'll work out. Anyway, you still got enough troubles of your own."

"Seems my troubles involving Vanita Lane and the diamonds are about over," Nudger said. "Now that she's dead."

"Nudge, Nudge. Think ahead, why don't you?"

Nudger had already done that, though not very far ahead. His mind was still working on the vision of Vanita sprawled dead on the blood-soaked mattress. He said, "I was probably the last person to see her alive, and I'll have to give a statement, but I was with Claudia all evening."

"Oh, you'll get through that part of it okay," Hammersmith said. "But let me tell you what we already know about Miss Lane's murder. She was viciously raped, probably by more than one man. Maybe even after death. There was semen in her mouth. You know how these things work; probably the autopsy'll reveal it in her rectal tract and vagina. There are also some cigarette burns on her nipples. And did you notice her hands?"

"Noticed something strange about them, yeah."

"Six of her fingers were broken. My point, Nudge, is she was tortured and then murdered by some very cold and nasty characters. We figure they were trying to get her to talk, at least at first. With the fingers. And after she gave up and talked is when they had their fun. And what worries me most is the way they killed her when they were finished using her. Very skillfully opened up a couple of major arteries so she'd spill her life out. Fast and efficient. Musta been casual. The way you'd bleed a farm animal to death. Like I said, cold types."

"But as soon as the diamonds are found—"

"The people they send to investigate airline disasters are experts. If there were diamonds near the point of that explosion, at least some of them would have been found by now. I can tell you that nothing like diamonds has been found. And didn't you say this Vanita Lane showed you your business card in your office? The card you gave her at the airport?"

"Right."

"Then she put it back in her purse?"

"I think so. Sure, she must have. She didn't give it back to me."

"We went through her purse, Nudge. And we searched that cottage with the thoroughness you only see at homicide scenes. Your card didn't turn up." Hammersmith shoved his cigar in his mouth. Blew smoke. Smiled around the cigar. "Know what that meansh?"

Nudger knew.

If his card wasn't in Vanita's purse or anywhere in the cottage, whoever killed her must have it. His stomach plunged. Found perilous equilibrium. Turned cold and shriveled with fear.

Hammersmith removed his cigar and stared at the ember

glowing fiery red in the night. "Cottage Thirteen, Nudge. Jesus! Why didn't you choose a luckier number?"

"I don't think that would have changed her luck."

"I was talking about *your* luck."

But Nudger knew it wasn't *13* that had landed him in this nightmare. It was *1,000.*

8

Hammersmith was right about Leo Springer. The ferretlike little captain personally conducted Nudger's interrogation at police headquarters at Tucker and Clark, hour after sweaty hour. Finally, after veiled threats and scathing insinuations, the police put Nudger on the street a few minutes after midnight. He felt as if his brain had been wrung out like a dishrag.

He crossed Clark toward the City Hall parking lot, where he'd left the Granada, and walked through an almost invisible cloud of tiny insects—gnats, maybe—that flitted about his eyes and nostrils. He was sure in the mood for that.

Even through the dark night he could see the traffic ticket stuck beneath the car's wiper. Nudger hadn't planned on being the subject of such a marathon interrogation, and time on the parking meter had long ago expired. He'd brought up the fact inside Headquarters that the meter needed feeding. Springer had given him an egg-sucking smile and said, "Amazing. Your ass is mixed up in a homicide and you're worried about getting a traffic ticket? Get your priorities straight, Nudger."

Well, Springer had been right. There'd been no need to worry. When Nudger yanked the slip of paper from beneath the wiper blade and studied it in the orangish hue of the overhead sodium lights, he saw that it wasn't a traffic ticket. It was a short note neatly printed in what looked like black felt-tip pen. "See you in your office tomorrow morning." It was signed "D.D.S."

Nudger stared at the initials. They usually stood for Doctor of Dental Surgery. He tried to remember if he owed his dentist any money. Couldn't be sure. No matter; dentists didn't often leave vaguely threatening notes on patients' cars. Most dentists. He remembered a movie he'd seen where a Nazi dentist tortured someone by drilling holes in his teeth without benefit of Novocaine. Yeow! The memory made him shiver.

He crumpled the note and stuffed it in his pocket, then withdrew his hand holding his keys and wearily got into the car. He sat without moving for a while to get reoriented after the isolation and intensity of hours under police pressure; innocent or guilty, nobody bounced back immediately after such a soul-smearing experience.

Then he drove through nearly deserted nighttime streets to his apartment. He locked himself in, and even made sure all the windows were locked. He was exhausted, had to get some sleep or he'd drop and become part of wherever he landed. Then he realized he'd worked up a thirst at Headquarters. He felt seriously dehydrated and probably was. The term "Sweat it out of them" was something Springer took literally, whether "it" was in them or in his own limited imagination.

Nudger got a Busch beer from the refrigerator and sat down on the sofa to drink it before going to bed, took a long pull on the can. He removed his shoes and let them thump on the floor, stretched his legs out straight and crossed them at the ankles. Gulping down some more of the cold beer, he felt it sting the back of his throat.

He backhanded a dribble of foam from his chin.

And fell asleep where he sat.

When he awoke, his lips were welded together and breath was rasping through his nose. His eyes were sealed, too, but he managed to raise his eyelids even though it felt as if they were on rusty hinges. The room was bright with morning. His head pressed to the pillow, he rolled a bleary eye toward his wristwatch.

Ten o'clock. Later than he usually slept.

And what was this? He was on the sofa and not in bed. Fully clothed except for his shoes, which were lying on their sides on the floor, toes angled toward each other. As if a pigeon-toed man had run right out of them.

He sat up, winced as pain sliced through his head, and remembered last night and how he'd fallen asleep on the sofa. He rocked forward slowly and looked down. The blue-and-white beer can lay near the shoes on the floor. The gray carpet was still damp where remaining beer had spilled out when the can fell from Nudger's hand. He couldn't remember dropping the can. He leaned farther forward and picked it up. A small amount of beer sloshed around hollowly in the bottom. The sound made Nudger nauseated.

After setting the can upright on an end table, he pushed himself to a standing position and aimed his body at the bathroom. He padded to it in his socks that had bunched down around his ankles during the night. Something cold seeped through the bottom of the right sock, and he realized he'd stepped in the damp spot on the carpet.

He hadn't dreamed. He was glad about that.

After a long, cool shower he felt better. But when he got dressed and went into the kitchen he discovered Mr. Coffee had joined the conspiracy against him and refused to work. He gnashed his teeth at the clear water in the glass pot, the gooey mass of grounds stuck in the filter. He'd give Mr. Coffee a medical exam tonight. The yellowing appliance was left over from his marriage and might have expired from old age. Nudger wasn't sure if he cared; it would give him a certain post-Eileen pleasure to chuck the balky appliance in the trash. It had never earned the right to be called *Mister*.

He drove in to work and found a delivery van being unloaded in front of the broken meter. It looked as if it would be parked there for quite a while, so he drove around the block and parked behind the doughnut shop. He locked the car and cut through the alleyway to the street. The stench of urine was strong in the alleyway. New graffiti said the end of the world was near. True for some people. When he reached the sidewalk, Danny noticed him through the greasy display window and motioned for him to come inside.

Nudger pushed in through the doughnut shop door. There was one customer at the stainless steel counter, an unkempt older man who looked like some kind of street person. He had a Dunker Delite on a napkin in front of him, and a glass of water. He looked as if he might be trying to build up his nerve about taking a bite of the doughnut, which was doubtless left over from yesterday; maybe it would be better to stay hungry.

"Got a guy waiting upstairs in your office, Nudge," Danny said, flicking at a fly on the counter with the grayish towel he always had tucked in his belt. The fly spiraled up and out of harm's way and was probably smiling at the clumsy human effort.

Nudger wasn't smiling, though. He experienced a flare of fear.

Then he decided that if one of the diamond thief/killers was waiting for him up in the office, he wouldn't have checked in with Danny. People plotting murder simply didn't act that way. Usually.

"Client?" Nudger asked, wondering if this was the D.D.S. who'd left the note on the Granada.

"Didn't say. Might be, though. He bought a Dunker Delite and took it up with him."

Great! Nudger might have another corpse on his hands. He didn't give voice to that thought; Danny was fiercely proud of his baking ability and sensitive about his cholesterol-packed product. Anybody who'd injure Danny's feelings would most likely kick a blind dog. "What's this guy look like?" Nudger asked. He usually got a brief rundown from Danny on whoever he'd directed upstairs to Nudger's office to wait.

Danny absently wiped his hands on the towel, as if they were wet. "Oh, I'd say a businessman type. Probably in his early forties. Nice suit. Carried a skinny little briefcase. Didn't seem nervous or anything. I seen him go in next door and heard him tromp upstairs and try your office door. Then he came back down and in here. Asked if I knew where you could be found. I told him you'd probably be here soon and asked if he wanted me to let him in the office to wait, just like you instructed about anybody who might be a client. He said sure and then he bought a Dunker Delite and coffee and I took him up and got him settled in the chair by your desk. Switched on the air conditioner so he wouldn't suffocate."

"How'd he seem?" Nudger asked. Danny sometimes displayed an innocent's clear insight into people.

"Comfortable enough, I'd say."

"Swell. How'd he seem in other ways?"

"Whaddaya mean?"

"He strike you as being angry or nervous or what?"

"None of them things. Just seemed . . . kinda normal."

"Like a Nazi dentist."

"Huh?"

"Never mind."

The old guy at the counter lurched down off his stool and went outside, carrying his doughnut in a white paper napkin. Body odor couldn't be overpowered even by the pungent, sugary aroma in the doughnut shop. Maybe he was a veteran and mention of the Nazis had scared him away. Or maybe he was the one who'd scrawled the end-of-the-world graffiti and didn't want to miss the show.

"Wanna cup of coffee, Nudge?"

Here were conflicting emotions. Nudger desperately needed some coffee, especially with a prospective client waiting upstairs, but the stuff Danny brewed in the complicated big steel urn was barely that. On the other hand, it did contain caffeine.

Nudger nodded. "Sure. Thanks, Danny."

Pleased, Danny twisted a valve near the base of the gigantic stainless steel urn. It hissed. Pipes snaking up the side of the thing made a gurgling sound. Black liquid oozed from a spiggot into a foam cup.

"Here you go, Nudge," Danny said, placing the cup on the counter. He bent over and reached into the glass display case. Plopped a Dunker Delite onto a napkin and set it next to the cup. "One of the fresh ones."

Nudger thanked Danny again. Then he said, "If I don't phone down here in half an hour, give the police a call, Danny."

Concern made Danny's basset-hound face fall to new sagginess. "Huh? You got some reason to be scared of this fella?"

"I don't think so, but you never know. Nudger wrapped the white napkin around the doughnut. What he'd created reminded him of a shroud-wrapped corpse. He picked up the weighty object in one hand, his cup of coffee in the other. Then he went upstairs to meet, most probably, the D.D.S. who'd left the note on his car last night. Thinking as he climbed the narrow steps about the Dropp Inn Motel. All that blood. How Vanita had been killed, what had been done to her so skillfully and dispassionately. D.D.S. Doctor of Diabolical Surgery?

Nudger's stomach lurched at the thought, and he almost dropped the Dunker Delite. But he kept climbing.

9

The man in the chair by Nudger's desk remained seated when Nudger entered the office. Glanced up. Finished chewing and swallowed a mouthful of Dunker Delite. Actually seemed to enjoy it. Said, "You Nudger?"

"Me," Nudger confirmed. He walked around and sat down behind the desk. The man didn't blink when the squealing swivel chair yowled at him. Maybe he'd tried it out before Nudger arrived.

He stood up to average height and brushed a few crumbs off his white shirt, not seeming to care if they fell on the floor. He was wearing a brown suit with almost indiscernible pin-stripes, a red tie with a knot the size of a fist. He reached in an inside pocket and withdrew a little leather case from which he snapped a fancy gold business card, and handed the card to Nudger. It was sticky from Dunker Delite icing, and it said the man's name was Bill Stockton and he was a representative of Sloan Trust Insurance.

Nudger placed the card on the desk, next to a battery-operated digital clock he'd received for subscribing to a magazine last year. The little plastic clock hadn't worked right for months; it flashed angular numerals from one through fifty-nine over and over, as if the earth were skipping on its axis and screwing up the passage of time.

He said, "Have a seat again, Mr. Stockton."

Stockton picked up his coffee from where he'd put it on the desk and sat back down. Crossed his legs. "Good coffee," he said. That put Nudger on his guard.

"Good doughnut, too," Nudger said, nodding toward the half-eaten Dunker Delite resting on a napkin next to where the coffee had been.

"Can't agree," the man said. Confusing.

Nudger pried the lid from his own foam coffee cup and set the cup on the vinyl edge of the desk pad. He didn't drink any, though. Had to build up to that.

Stockton had a round face with small brown eyes and a tiny, thin-lipped mouth. A short but hawkish nose made him somewhat resemble a puffed-up bird. He smiled and revealed miniature sharp teeth, the kind birds would have if they had teeth. He said, "Diamonds, Mr. Nudger."

"Which and what about?"

"Stolen diamonds I've been trying to recover for my insurance company for the past month and a half. That's which diamonds. The what-about-them part is that my search has led me here." He glanced around the office.

Nudger decided to be careful. What did this guy know? Nudger had run across insurance investigators before, and some of them were tricky as Houdini in their pursuit of percentage. He said, "I never stole any diamonds, Mr. Stockton."

"Nope, not that I know about. But you did have as a client one Vanita Lane, who was murdered last night at the Dropp Inn Motel."

"Ah, you read the morning paper."

"Didn't have to," Stockton said. "I knew about Vanita Lane hiring you, and I went by the motel last night after the police had arrived. What I'm doing here is asking what Vanita Lane told you about the diamonds."

It was no longer a secret among insiders. Nudger decided to level. "She said they were on the plane that blew up at the airport two days ago."

"Not so."

"Not so that she said that?"

"That the diamonds were on the airliner."

"Maybe they haven't been found yet," Nudger suggested.

"My guess is they were never on the plane."

"She said differently."

Stockton laughed. He sipped his coffee as if he needed some to keep from choking on his amusement at the roundabout and evasive conversation. "Crude as it is to speak ill of the dead, Mr. Nudger, Vanita Lane was a woman who'd tell anyone anything that suited her. Even sometimes if it didn't suit her. She was a pathological liar."

Nudger saw hope here. "You mean she really had nothing to do with the diamond theft?"

"Oh, she had enough to do with it. Knew about it beforehand and said nothing. She and Rupert Winslow were lovers."

"She told me about the relationship with Winslow. Also said things between them had cooled down."

"That's not the story I got from people at the Meridian Hotel in New York, where she spent most of last week with him wearing out a bed."

Nudger did sample his coffee now. Aww! Terrible! Maybe something had crawled into the urn and died. "She didn't tell me that."

"Well, like I said, she's selective. But if she told you Winslow was a murder victim instead of a suicide, she was speaking the truth there."

"She was scared," Nudger said.

"Was she?"

"Yeah. She wasn't faking that."

Stockton gave his itty-bitty smile. "Neither are you, I bet."

"You mean because the thieves might think I have the diamonds?"

Stockton shrugged. "If you see it as a possibility, they must, too."

Nudger squeaked back and forth in his swivel chair. "What about you? How do you see it?"

"Well, Vanita Lane was more than just a liar. She used sex any way she could in order to get what she wanted. Something Rupert Winslow didn't care about, because often what she wanted was what he told her to want. But she was plenty promiscuous on her own. 'Nymphomaniac' isn't too strong a word." A confidential leer. "How 'bout it, Mr. Nudger? You get it on with Vanita Lane?"

Nudger stared hard at Stockton. He kept his tone casual, though. "Naw. I don't generally do that with my clients. Do you?"

"Sometimes. I think maybe when Winslow was killed Vanita got scared and hired you to take care of her and the diamonds. Used sex to make the arrangement more intimate and reliable. That'd fit her pattern."

Nudger was getting tired of this. And more uneasy by the minute. "There was no sex and no diamonds. Which means I'm out of this affair."

"That would be living in a fool's paradise, Mr. Nudger. But not for very long. Better believe the people who stole these diamonds are the type who'd do anything necessary to get the truth outa you. Me, I'm bound by ethics and the law, so I can only politely inquire."

"She told me the diamonds were on the plane," Nudger said. "When I took the case I figured they'd be found by the crash-site investigators and get mentioned in the news. At that point my job'd be over."

"But they weren't found and aren't going to be. And you're in big trouble with some very dangerous folks. Only thing that *will* keep them off your back now is the news that the diamonds have been recovered and returned to their rightful owner. Which means your way to continued health and long life is to hand them over to me."

"I would if I had them."

"They're worth approximately a million dollars, Mr. Nudger, but they're worthless if you're not around to spend the money. What's Rupert Winslow buying these days? Does Vanita Lane figure to go shopping again?"

Nudger picked up his foam cup, started to sip, then put it down and shoved it away. "You really think I've got those diamonds?"

"Honestly, I don't know. But if you do have them, or know where they are, do us both a favor and get them to me. You're in deep and dangerous waters, Mr. Nudger, and I'm your life preserver."

Nudger said, "You make me wish I did have them or knew where to get them. But I don't."

Stockton stared at him for a while in the way a person looks at an inanimate object, such as a laid-out corpse. Finally he said, "Too bad," and stood up. "If you need to get in touch with me, I'm staying downtown at the Clarion Hotel. Or you can call the number on my card and the company'll forward a message."

Nudger picked up the card again and looked at a 212 area code. New York, he was pretty sure.

Stockton buttoned his suitcoat and walked to the door. Sort of strutted, actually. He turned and said, "You take care," and then went out.

Nudger listened to him clomp down the stairs. Heard the street door clatter open and closed.

He sat for a long time in the swivel chair, gazing out the window and thinking about what Stockton had said, wondering how much of it he should believe.

Vanita hadn't seemed nymphomaniacal. If she had been, surely she'd have put some moves on Nudger there in the motel. Surely.

Stockton was on target about one thing: It was probable that whoever was searching for the diamonds might think they were in Nudger's possession.

Might try to get them back. *Gulp!*

A pigeon flapped down and perched on the window ledge.

It puffed out its chest and stared in at Nudger. Something in its mocking gaze seemed to be goading him to take action. It looked remarkably like Stockton.

Nudger didn't know what to do, but he had to do something.

He looked down at the calendar desk pad, where a name was scribbled in the margin.

Marcy Lou Dee. Vanita's baby sister, Marlou.

Nudger picked up a ballpoint pen and drew a circle around the name.

It was time to talk with Marlou.

10

Finding Marlou Dee's address provided Nudger the opportunity for a little genuine detective work. But very little, as there was only one M. L. Dee in the phone book.

Nudger dropped the directory back in the desk drawer with a *thunk!* and shoved the drawer closed. He stared at Marlou's address and phone number he'd scrawled on the back of a Publishers Clearinghouse Sweepstakes envelope he'd retrieved from the wastebasket.

He decided it might be better not to phone first, but to go directly to where she lived and try to talk with her; he couldn't be sure what or how much she knew about her sister's business and romantic life, or how much she'd be willing to tell, and it might be better to catch her unprepared. That way, if she lied, it would be less imaginative and more obvious.

He told Danny he was leaving for a while, then got in the Granada and drove down Manchester to Chouteau and turned south on Grand. Brilliant sunlight struck the windshield and penetrated the car as heat. The air conditioner tried hard but couldn't cope.

Nudger's hands were slippery with sweat on the steering wheel by the time he reached Shenandoah, Marlou Dee's street. He drove a few depressing blocks and parked in sun-dappled shade across from the brick, tar-roofed, four-family building that bore her address like a grudge.

This was a rough section of town that was undergoing early stages of renovation. Gentrification hadn't quite set in and real estate was still cheap; the renovators were still bringing the rows of similar old brick buildings up to code so they'd qualify under a city plan for subsidized low-rental units. The street was racially mixed, though it seemed to be occupied mostly by poorer white families, some of them not far removed from the country. A lot of the lower-floor windows of the rehabbed buildings were equipped with iron grillwork to keep out intruders. The early-bird urban pioneers who'd moved into the area knew the score and were being careful while biding their time waiting for property values to rise, hoping they'd guessed right.

Nudger locked his car and crossed the street toward Marlou's building. It needed tuck-pointing, and the green paint on the gutters and window frames was peeling. There was a slanted metal awning over the cracked concrete porch. A circling squadron of wicked-looking wasps droned overhead, up near the sun-heated awning, threatening to break formation at any moment and peel off like fighter planes to dive at Nudger.

He saw Marlou's name beneath the doorbell button of the second-floor-east unit. Pressed the button and waited, glancing upward now and then at the lazily maneuvering wasps. Thinking, if there really was a god, why would He have created such insects? But then, He'd created pigeons.

After a minute or so he heard someone descending the steps on the other side of the age-checked door. A floorboard creaked.

The door swung inward, and a woman wearing tight Levi's and a baggy white blouse stared out at him. She was average height, maybe even on the short side, but a kind of lankiness made her seem taller. About thirty, she had carrot-colored hair, wide green eyes, and a tiny nose that didn't quite turn up. She didn't have the complexion you usually saw with red hair. Her skin was creamy and not a freckle was evident except for a light dusting across the bridge of her nose. She was barefoot; her feet were small, with short, squarish toes, and they were dirty, as if she'd been walking through dust. She cocked her head at him, waiting for him to speak. He noticed her eyes were red-rimmed. She'd been crying.

"Marlou Dee?"

She looked puzzled. Pursed her full lips and kept them that way for a few seconds before deciding to answer. Slightly protruding front teeth kept them from meeting all the way. "Mostly it's only family and friends call me that."

"Your sister, Vanita, told me you went by that name. I'm sorry about what happened."

Marlou studied him, something sad in those wide green eyes. "I just come back from the morgue," she said. "I identified Vanita's . . . Identified her." For a second the flesh beneath her eyes danced, then she took a deep breath and regained control. "You gotta excuse me," she said. "I'm still a mite shook up."

Nudger had to resist the compulsion to hug her and pat her head, assure her that grief would lift and life would eventually brighten. She had about her a kind of child-woman vulnerability and probably would have all her life. What he did was stand there awkwardly and say, "Musta been rough."

She smiled morosely, revealing a wide gap between her front teeth, and shook her head. "Wasn't so bad as I feared, actually. Almost like looking at somebody else. I still gotta remind myself Vanita's gone. We didn't see each other much, but we was close enough."

"She told me you two were close."

"Did she? Why?"

"She hired me to help her."

"Whaddaya mean, 'help her'?"

"She was afraid."

Marlou squinted suspiciously. It caused her nose to crinkle and made her look like a twelve-year-old. "You ain't some friend of Rupert's, are you?"

"No, I'm a private investigator. Name's Nudger." He showed her his ID. She didn't seem at all impressed by meeting a real-life private detective.

Marlou sniffled, then wiped her nose by running her palm over it straight up, the way preschool kids wipe their noses; she was looking younger all the time. "Well, it turned out Vanita had good cause to be scared, wouldn't you say?"

"I'd say. The police tell you anything about why she mighta been killed?"

Marlou's eyes got wider. Warier, too. "No. I, like, figured she was murdered by some kinda sex maniac or something. Nobody I talked to told me otherwise. Nobody told me much of anything, actually. Just asked questions. Asked and asked." Her entire body gave a little twitching motion, as if she'd suddenly come fully awake. "What'm I thinking, letting you stand out there in the heat. Seems my mind's gone on vacation. C'mon in, Mr. Nudger."

He followed her up a flight of rubber-matted wooden steps to her second-floor flat. It had been painted white recently; there were fresh speckles on the hardwood floor. The furniture was a worn-looking hodgepodge. A braided oval rug was centered on the living room floor, and an old-fashioned tarnished brass chandelier dangled crookedly from the ceiling. The living room had a small marble fireplace with a bent piece of cardboard crammed into its opening. It wasn't much cooler inside the flat than it had been out on the porch.

Despite the humbleness of the furnishings, the place was neatly arranged and clean and exuded a kind of hominess. There was a St. Louis Cardinals coffee cup, half full, on the table next to the sagging green sofa. On one wall homemade bookcases contained rows of paperbacks, many of them romances. Maybe Marlou dreamed about a Heathcliffe type on a white stallion scooping her up and galloping with her west on Shenandoah toward the wealthy suburbs and into a new life. Or some variation thereof, such as a guy with a steady job and a paid-for white Chevy. Marlou's was a K mart kind of world.

"Please siddown, Mr. Nudger." She motioned toward a faded wing chair facing the sofa. "Cuppa coffee?"

"No, thanks, I already had mine this morning." He sat. Felt a spring probe his right buttock. He shifted his weight and got comfortable. Sort of. "What kinda questions the police ask you?"

She sat down in a corner of the sofa, then picked up the Cardinals cup and sipped. "They wanted to know how well I knew Rupert. I told them hardly at all, which is the God's truth. Only met the creep, like, three or four times, when he was with Vanita." The mention of her sister's name caused her eyes to cloud. She swiped at them with the back of her hand. Then she took another swallow of coffee and set the cup down on the table. She looked desolate and said, "God, it don't seem real. None of it does."

Nudger brought her back to the subject of Rupert, away from her sorrow. "Why do you say he was a creep?"

Her narrow shoulders rose and fell in a shrug. "Heck, five minutes with him and you could tell he was pure phony. He lied to Vanita more'n once, I can tell you. Had her starry-eyed and fooled, though, and she'd be ready to believe the next lie. She called him Ropes 'stead of Rupert, for some reason. Most everybody could see through him like he was cheap bologna. 'Cept for Vanita. Love really is blind, I guess."

"Sometimes mute, too. A tragic combination."

"Why, that really is wise, Mr. Nudger. You oughta be a philosopher 'stead of a detective."

Now that she thought he was wise as Plato, Nudger decided to be direct. "You know about the diamonds?"

She didn't react much. "Nope. Whichever diamonds do you mean?"

"Didn't the police mention them?"

She was wearing a puzzled expression. Very faint lines formed on her broad forehead. "Diamonds? No, sir. Why?"

Nudger realized he was mucking around in an active homicide investigation, something Springer had explicitly warned him about. But it wasn't Springer who might be suspected by killer thieves of possessing what they wanted. Nudger had to protect himself. He said, "It could be that whoever killed Vanita thought she had some diamonds."

The innocent, gap-toothed grin. Incredulous. "Vanita weren't no more rich than I am. Mosta that stuff she had was gave to her or financed over the next thousand years. If she had diamonds, you can bet she had payments to go with 'em."

"Stolen diamonds," Nudger said.

Marlou said, "Oh!" And then, "Rupert. That bastard Rupert got her killed."

Nudger said, "Could be."

"This have something to do with Rupert blowing up that airplane?"

"Everything to do with it," Nudger said.

"Well, best you tell me about it."

Nudger hesitated, then he figured Stockton would get to Marlou soon enough, and maybe the police wouldn't ask who'd told her first about Rupert and the diamonds.

Screw Springer and his warnings.

Nudger drew a deep breath. He told Marlou about her dead sister, and how Rupert Winslow and twice-stolen diamonds and the people looking for those diamonds had made her that way.

||

After leaving the Granada parked by the broken meter, Nudger dodged traffic and jogged across sun-baked pavement toward his office. Heat radiating from the street swirled around his ankles and worked its way up his pants legs. As he hopped up onto the sidewalk to safety, he saw the man inside the doughnut shop swivel down off his stool.

He'd been watching Nudger, waiting for him to get across Manchester. Beyond the man, who was now moving toward the door, the white-aproned figure of Danny gave a helpless little shrug. *No time to warn you, Nudge.*

Eileen's lawyer, Henry Mercato, pushed open the doughnut shop door and stepped outside into the sun. He was a short man whose stomach paunch seemed somehow to be masculine and pugnacious, like an outthrust chest. He was wearing a pinstriped blue suit and vest, red-and-blue striped tie, gleaming black wingtip shoes. His lawyer's uniform. His black hair was, as always, speckled with dandruff, some of which was on the shoulders of the blue suit. He was grinning at Nudger, the flesh around the corners of his dark eyes—fierce as a cannibal's—

crinkled. His teeth were white and perfect, his skin was flawless, his hair was greased down and neatly combed, parted near the middle. He was groomed like a department store mannequin, except for that dandruff.

Anticipating Nudger's reaction, he didn't bother extending his hand. "Mr. Nudger, we need to talk."

Nudger slid his own hands in his pockets. "About Eileen?"

Still showing his underslung, sharklike grin, Mercato nodded.

"I explained to her I'd pay what I owe," Nudger said. "Just takes time."

Mercato stopped grinning. Something sparkled in his dark eyes. "Lotta time's already passed."

Nudger was getting uncomfortable, and not just from the sun bearing down hotly on the back of his neck. He didn't feel like a bout of vicious repartee with Henry Mercato. "You here to serve a summons or something?" Nudger asked.

"You know I don't do that kinda thing, Mr. Nudger. Experience shoulda taught you, court's got other means to summon you."

"So what do you want?" Nudger asked.

"I'll tell you, but it's gonna take more time than I'd like to spend standing here in the heat."

Nudger sighed. "Okay, c'mon up."

He opened the street door and trudged up the narrow wooden stairs to his office door. Removed the handwritten BACK SOON. SEE DOUGHNUT SHOP PROPRIETER DOWNSTAIRS sign from the office door and shoved the door open, then stood aside so Mercato could enter.

"Phew!" Mercato said. "Hotter in here than outside. Smells funny, too."

"Doughnuts."

"Yeah, that's right." As if he'd asked Nudger to guess.

Nudger dropped the cardboard sign on the desk and switched on the air conditioner. Something was wrong with it; beneath the usual watery hum it was going *pinka pinka pinka pinka.* Maybe the fan hitting something.

He said, "It won't take long to cool down." He sat down behind the desk. *Eeeek!* Didn't invite Mercato to sit. Swiveled slowly back and forth. *Eeek! Pinka pinka pinka. Eeek! Pinka pinka pinka.*

Mercato stood perfectly at ease, though a trickle of perspiration was tracking down the left side of his neck toward his white collar. It disappeared inside the collar. He said, "I'm here at the request of Ms. Vogel in regard to the back alimony you owe her."

Nudger sat still. *Ms. Vogel?* He didn't realize who Mercato was talking about at first. It took a few seconds for it to hit him: Eileen's maiden name. He knew Mercato and felt like throwing this little chaser of skirts and ambulances out of the office, but Mercato had behind him the power of due process. Of The Law. Politely, Nudger said, "I explained to her that when I could afford it—"

"Sure, sure." Mercato waved a hand, causing a gold ring to glint in the light streaming through the dirty window. "The thing is, Eil—Ms. Vogel, has reason to believe you *can* afford to pay, and that you're misusing funds that should otherwise be directed to her account."

Nudger felt his stomach kick. "Oh, she's so right, Henry! That's why I'm living in a *chic* apartment over on Sutton and working out of this plush office." *Pinka pinka pinka.* "Where's Eileen living now? Out in Frontenac, right? House with a pool?"

"She needs the pool for therapeutic reasons. Back trouble."

"From moving around her money?"

"No sense getting irrational, Nudger."

"*Irrational?* You know what they say about blood and the turnip? Well, I'm the turnip, and she knows it. What the hell's Eileen want outa me?"

"Only what you legally owe her."

"Same way with the electric company and my landlord. I give her what's left, Henry. What's still in my pocket after I've done what I can to keep a roof over me and some generic food in the refrigerator."

"Law's not interested in what brand soup you eat, Nudger,

even if it's no brand. The law's interested in the fact you got money to spend lavishly on women and dining out while you poor-mouth your former spouse. The fact that you work outa this crummy hole isn't fooling anybody. You ain't so stupid as to lease a fancy office in Clayton. And the business you're in, you don't need to put up any kind of front. Mosta your clients probably come from the lower classes anyway."

"What women? What lavish dining out?"

"A certain Claudia Bettencourt is a woman, right?"

"Better believe."

"Ms. Vogel saw you and her at Al Baker's having prime rib and wine no more'n a month ago. One of the best restaurants in town, and far from the cheapest. Least it's not so reasonably priced that you had money left over to write Ms. Vogel's monthly check, which was due the very next day."

So that was it. "That was an exception," Nudger said. "Clau—Ms. Bettencourt had undergone medical tests that indicated she might have cancer. Later, when we found out she was perfectly healthy, we celebrated. Didn't go on a cruise, just had dinner out. If Eileen doesn't like it, the hell with her."

The air conditioner hadn't caught up with the heat yet. *Pinka Pinka.* Mercato's face was red. He was warming up inside and out. "What she doesn't like translates into money you better pay her, Nudger. Tell you something, it was my suggestion she just haul you into court, get a judgment against you for back alimony and petition to have your monthly payments increased. She can do it with no trouble at all; like snatching money from a blind paperboy. She's the one said why don't I come talk reasonably to you, give you a fucking chance."

"Save herself some legal fees, you mean. Or do you charge her, what with the occasional sleep-in arrangement you have with my former wife?"

Mercato's fierce dark eyes bulged. "Ms. Vogel's social life's got nothing to do with business."

"Mine, either."

Mercato shook his head. "This is exactly why I advised her

to have a shit-for-brains like you summoned right to court. Not screw around with this kinda Michael Mouse conversation."

"So consider the conversation over, Henry. Go away."

"Another thing," Mercato said, ignoring the fact that Nudger had pointedly opened a desk drawer and was pretending to search for very important papers; something to do with his hands, anyway. "I don't believe you when you say you can't afford to pay what you owe."

For an instant Nudger wondered if Mercato could somehow know about the missing diamonds and think Nudger had them.

No, impossible. Nothing about diamonds had hit the news. Everyone from the police to the insurance company wanted the lid kept on as long as possible.

"You got clients, Nudger. I read in the papers one of them just got killed."

"Which means she doesn't sign checks anymore," Nudger said in a level voice. "Bye, Henry."

"You'll be hearing from—"

"Your lawyer?"

"From the law, fuckface!" Mercato drew himself to full height and tugged down on the lapels of his suitcoat simultaneously with both hands, like a ham actor playing an old-time politician who'd just made a dynamite speech. He strode toward the door.

"Henry." Nudger stopped him before he stepped out onto the landing. "Get yourself a better tailor; your dorsal fin's showing."

Mercato started to spit back an answer, then seemed to change his mind. A looseness came over his Napoleonic little form. *Hard to imagine him in bed with Eileen.* He said, "My dorsal fin's showing like that noose around your neck's showing. And the best thing is, you'll pull it tight yourself. Guys like you always do." He let his grin spread and walked out. Closed the door behind him very gently, so it made the softest click that could be heard between the *pinka pinka pinka.*

Nudger continued rooting through the drawer until he remembered he'd only begun doing it to make Mercato think he was preoccupied. He wasn't searching for anything.

He slid the drawer shut, then reached back and slapped the air conditioner. The strange pinking noise stopped. Maybe Mercato had somehow caused it. Mechanical things reacted negatively to certain people; Nudger knew this because he was one of them.

He opened another drawer, got out a fresh roll of antacid tablets, and peeled back the silver foil. Chomped a couple of the chalky disks, listening to the muted sound of them breaking up between his molars, and thought about what Henry Mercato had said about the noose.

He knew there was a touch of truth to it.

12

Nudger said, "Stuffed flounder."

Claudia stood in the doorway to the kitchen holding two frozen dinners, still in their boxes.

"Unless you'd rather have it tomorrow instead of the ravioli," he added.

"I told you," Claudia said, "it doesn't make any difference to me. But my hands are getting cold, Nudger. Make up your mind so I can get one of these into the microwave." She had to go to a parent-faculty spaghetti dinner out at Stowe School tonight, so he was eating alone. She glanced at the clock in the dining room. "I've gotta get out of here in twenty minutes or I'll be late."

"Make it the flounder, then," Nudger said. "The flounder definitely." She turned and disappeared into the kitchen. The moment he'd said flounder, he'd developed a yearning for Italian food. Ravioli. She wouldn't understand if he changed his mind again. He'd better stay with the flounder. Take it out of its cardboard tray when it was done and put it on a dish. Have some white wine with it. Just like a real meal.

He got up from his chair and walked into the kitchen. The light was on in the microwave and air was whooshing out its vents. He could see the flounder inside. It didn't look bad. He sat down at the kitchen table and said, "Henry Mercato was by to see me today."

"That little cutthroat lawyer?"

"Yeah." He watched her turn on the sink faucet and rinse her hands. "Seems Eileen saw us eating at Al Baker's Restaurant last month. That's what started this latest campaign for higher alimony."

"You tell him we eat there at least once a decade?"

"No reason to tell him. He knows it."

"If Eileen needs the money so badly, what was she doing at Al Baker's?"

There was something Nudger wished he'd thought to ask Mercato.

"I teach school," Claudia said, drying her hands on a plaid dish towel. "You do . . . what you do. How on earth can Eileen make a case that you should pay her more? She recently bought a bigger house, didn't she?"

"With a pool. Mercato said she needs that for therapeutic reasons. Her back."

"Her back, huh. She probably—" Claudia bit off her words and stared in at the flounder.

"What?"

"Nothing," she said. She opened the microwave's door, spun the flounder a quarter turn, and reset the timer. Liquid diode numerals said Nudger was going to eat in six minutes. "I've gotta get ready to leave," Claudia said. "Can you keep an eye on this fish?"

"Sure."

Claudia went into the bedroom to change, and Nudger sat staring at the seconds being marked off on the microwave. He could smell the flounder now. It didn't smell as good as it looked, but then fish never did.

He decided there was time to use the beeperless remote to check his answering machine for messages. Turned in his chair so he could reach the wall phone. He punched out his office number, then the code that activated the machine on the other end of the line. Man calling microchip.

Beep! "Hi! Mr. Nudger, this is your friend Chris. If you're interested in winning a brand-new Toyota just for visiting . . ."

Nudger stopped listening to Chris, whom he'd never met. There was no way to fast-forward the machine over the phone, so he sat patiently through the rest of the Toyota–lakeside resort pitch. Then a spirited threat from Eileen. Then someone who wanted to sell him a cemetery plot. Or was that Eileen calling back and disguising her voice?

Beep! "Mr. Nudger, this is Marlou Dee." He immediately picked up the tension in her voice. "There was this man standing out in the street watching my apartment. I closed the curtains, but when I looked outside he was still there. About five minutes ago he came right up and knocked on my door, but I didn't answer. He went back outside and he's sitting in a car now, like he's waiting for somebody. Something, like, creepy about him—"

She'd run out of time on the machine.

Beep! "You can win two fun-filled weeks in Jamaica just by answering—"

Nudger hung up. Got Claudia's phone directory from its drawer and looked up Marlou's number again. He went back to the phone and pecked the number out carefully with his forefinger.

Her phone rang five times. Nudger knew if a phone wasn't picked up by the fifth ring the odds of it being answered became very long indeed.

He waited four more rings, then pressed down the phone's cradle button and called Hammersmith. He told him about Marlou Dee and the message on the answering machine. As soon as Hammersmith got her address, he hung up.

Nudger punched the Off button on the microwave and hurried toward the bedroom. Claudia wasn't there. She was in the bathroom with the door closed. He knocked lightly and said, "I've gotta go, Claudia."

"I'm about to step into the shower."

"I mean I've gotta leave. Get someplace in a hurry on business and meet Hammersmith. Can you put that flounder back in the freezer?"

There was an eruption of water under pressure in the bathroom as she turned on the shower. Maybe she answered him and he couldn't hear over the sound of the blasting water. He didn't have time to wait and find out. Yelled good-bye to her and got out of there.

Marlou's apartment was only fifteen minutes away from Claudia's. When Nudger got there Hammersmith hadn't arrived, but there was a police car at the curb. It's roofbar lights were off, so no neighbors had gathered. Or was that because in this neighborhood people automatically tended to shy away from police cars.

Nudger parked the Granada behind the cruiser and got out. As he entered the building, an image of Vanita at the Dropp Inn Motel flashed on the screen of his mind and he had to force himself to move fast up the stairs toward Marlou's apartment. He wanted to get there but didn't want to be there.

Christ, what he might see!

Her door was standing open. Nudger heard voices from inside. Saw a blue-uniformed elbow. It occurred to him that maybe Bill Stockton had discovered Vanita had a sister, and that he was the man who'd been watching Marlou's apartment and then knocked on her door. It was possible. If Stockton hadn't already known about Marlou, he might have found out. Might even have followed Nudger to her apartment the first time, learned about her that way.

Nudger stepped into the apartment. A man was braced against the wall while a uniform held a gun on him. He was leaning forward at an extreme angle, his feet spread wide and his hands splayed against the plaster. As if the wall were pushing back.

He wasn't Stockton. He looked vaguely familiar, but Nudger couldn't place him.

Another uniform, with his revolver holstered, turned toward Nudger. "Hold it right there."

Nudger froze in the doorway. Said, "I'm the one called the police. Where's Marlou?"

"Where's who?"

"The woman who lives here."

The cop holding the gun on the man braced against the wall said, "She's in the bedroom."

Vanita had died in bed at the Dropp Inn Motel.

Nudger plodded through his fear toward the bedroom door. The other uniform told him to stop but he barely heard. *He might be the one responsible for this.*

He was aware of the uniform moving toward him as he reached the bedroom door.

"I wouldn't go in there if I was you, pal."

But Nudger ignored the cop's warning. Gulped. Flung the door open.

Marlou said, "Oh!"

She was standing with her Levi's unzipped and had a black T-shirt stretched between her arms, about to work it over her head. She wasn't wearing a bra.

As soon as she recovered from her surprise, she crammed her head through the shirt's neck and yanked it down so violently she almost tore it. The only body on the bed was that of an inanely grinning Raggedy Ann doll propped against a pillow. It seemed to be laughing at Nudger.

He said, "I—uh, I'm sorry. I got your message and tried to phone. Didn't get an answer."

She smiled. "S'okay, Mr. Nudger. That man I told you about, him and I got into a kind of argument in the hall. When I tried to get back inside and answer my phone, he wouldn't let me. Said he wasn't finished talking to me."

"The man the cops have got in the living room?"

"Yep."

"You mean he physically kept you from going back into your apartment to answer your phone?"

"Not exactly. He more like threatened."

—— 79 ——

"What were you arguing about?"

"You ain't gonna believe—"

"This guy a friend?" The uniform who'd warned Nudger not to open the bedroom door had come in. He was glaring at Nudger.

"Sure is. No problem, Officer."

The uniform looked confused, shrugged, then swaggered from the bedroom. He left the door standing open.

Nudger started to drift after him. Marlou straightened the twisted T-shirt. It had one of those yellow smiley faces on it, right over her breasts. Nudger tried not to think about that as she followed him into the living room.

The guy who'd been braced against the wall was standing up straight now, and the other uniform had replaced his revolver in its holster. But he had his nightstick resting lightly in his right hand, as if he could use it in a second.

There was a noise on the landing and the obese but graceful Hammersmith glided in. Fat but sleek, like a seal under water.

Both uniforms recognized him and stood taller and put on their professional faces. Just this side of being bored, but very alert. The one holding the nightstick said, "He was banging on the door when we got here, Lieutenant."

"This one?" Hammersmith asked, staring at Nudger with a mean, amused glint in his eye.

"No, sir, not him. He's a friend or something of the woman who lives here. This one"—he nodded toward the man standing and looking embarrassed—"a Mr. Edward Franks. Woman who lives here, a Mizz Marcy Lou Dee, says he used threatening and abusive language toward her."

Nudger studied Franks, who was a middle-aged, paunchy man with his shirt twisted up and unbuttoned in front from when he was braced against the wall with his arms raised. His navel was visible. There was lint in it. Franks had thinning sandy hair and rheumy-looking blue eyes. A fleshy, mottled face. Though he seemed embarrassed, he didn't look fearful or dangerous. Not like a proper cornered diamond thief and killer.

Hammersmith said, "Tell me about him."

—— 80 ——

One of the uniforms said, "Mr. Franks is a private investigator. Says he's doing work for a law firm. Whazza firm, Franks?"

Franks said, "Schlozzel, Barnes and Schlozzel."

The uniform was taking notes now in his leather-bound pad. "That with two Z's?"

"And a C."

The uniform looked puzzled, then finished writing and flipped his notepad shut.

Nudger was no longer puzzled. Henry Mercato was a partner at Schlozzel, Barnes and Schlozzel.

Franks said, "I was only trying to ask Miss Dee about her connection with this case I'm on."

"What kind of case?" Hammersmith asked.

Franks glanced at Nudger. "I'm trying to establish that our client's former husband is spending an unreasonable amount of time and money on women instead of making his alimony payments."

Hammersmith had it now. He shook his head so that his smooth pink jowels quivered. "And your client is?"

Franks said, "Schloz—"

"And *their* client?"

"They might want that confidential, Lieutenant."

Nudger said, "It's Eileen, Jack."

Everyone stared at him.

"That little bastard Mercato's having me and Claudia watched. Franks probably followed me here earlier today and figured it wasn't a business call."

"Only trying to find out," Franks said apologetically. "My job. There was no reason for the lady to get so excited."

"She thought you might be somebody else," Hammersmith said. "So'd the rest of us. That's why Nudger phoned me when he learned a strange man was menacing Miss Dee."

"Somebody else?"

Hammersmith said, "You goddamn blundered into the middle of a homicide investigation, Franks."

Franks's pinkish eyes took on a sickly sheen. "Jesus,

Lieutenant, I had no idea the lady was off-limits. How could I have?"

Hammersmith ignored the question. "Mercato the one who hired you?"

"That's right," Franks said. Eager to cooperate now. A homicide case.

"You follow Nudger here earlier? That what set you onto Miss Dee?"

"That's it. I was told to check things out when he saw other women. That's all I was doing. Just my job."

"You already told us that." Hammersmith frowned at Franks. "You used to be a cop, didn't you?"

"Yeah, for a while. Second District."

Nudger remembered now. Franks had been forced to resign three or four years ago after roughing up the black wife of a fire chief. Mistook her for a woman wanted on a bad-check charge. Franks had made racial remarks. Then, in an interview, he'd lost his composure and made the same remarks to the press and defended his prejudice. So now he was in Nudger's line of work. Great.

Franks stood up straighter. "I'd appreciate any cooperation from the police in this matter, Lieutenant." Getting haughty now. Going on the offensive, even if feebly.

Hammersmith pulled one of his greenish cigars from his shirt pocket, then removed the cellophane wrapper and crammed the cigar in his mouth. He looked hard at Franks and said quite clearly around the cigar, "Go away."

After Franks had hurried out and clomped down the stairs to the street door, Hammersmith told the two uniforms they could return to their car and call back into service. Then he wandered over to the window and gazed outside. He said, "I didn't know you were aware of Miss Dee's existence, Nudge."

"Her sister told me about her."

Hammersmith, still with the unlit cigar in his mouth, turned around and faced Marlou. Said, "That how it went? This Franks question you about Nudger?"

She said, "Yep. And he got downright insistent that there was something going on. I mean, like in a romantic way between me and Mr. Nudger."

Hammersmith snorted. "Wouldn't be the first time Franks arranged to find what he set out for."

Marlou smiled her blue-skies-and-waving-wheat smile and said, "S'okay by me if you smoke in here, Lieutenant."

Nudger thought, God, no! You shouldn't have told him that.

But Hammersmith was smiling benignly at Marlou and already had his lighter out. Within half a minute he was emitting more air pollution than the Hertz fleet.

Marlou didn't seem to mind the greenish haze. She said, "I was watching Mr. Franks watch *me* for the last hour or so. Then I just had to get to the funeral parlor where Vanita's gonna be laid out. But when I started to change clothes there was this knock on the door (*So she'd been* removing *the T-shirt when Nudger interrupted her*) and . . . well, he knew I'd ignored his knock before, so when he came back anyway, I got mad. Decided to answer it and tell him to leave me alone whoever he was."

"Didn't you realize he might be the one who killed your sister?" Hammersmith asked.

"It was only possible," Marlou said calmly, "not, like, definite."

Nudger decided both Dee sisters were born with more nerve than was good for them.

Hammersmith inhaled. Blew out green thunderclouds. "You wanna bring a complaint against Franks? Disturbing your peace? Threatening to do great bodily harm? Whatever?"

"Would it do any good?"

"Naw. But I think he'll leave you alone, now that he knows you haven't succumbed to Nudger's charms."

Marlou glanced at Nudger. Did she blush?

Hammersmith said, "I gotta go, Nudge. Miss Dee, there anything else?"

"Nope, Lieutenant. And I do appreciate you sending somebody here so fast."

Hammersmith beamed, blew more smoke, and glided out of the apartment.

Nudger looked at Marlou, who was grinning at him like the Raggedy Ann doll. "After what happened to Vanita, I sure was scared."

"You didn't seem so scared," Nudger said. "You went to the door the second time."

A certain light entered her green eyes. "I got Dee blood in me, Mr. Nudger. That means I get pushed only so far, then I turn around and push back. Sorta automatically. Means I'm cursed with a fiery kinda temper sometimes gets the better of sound judgment."

Nudger smiled. "I'll remember that, Marlou. Has a man named Bill Stockton been to see you?"

"Oh, sure. That insurance guy. He was by here 'bout an hour after you left. I didn't like the way he talked about Vanita. Didn't like *him*, either. He put me in mind of Heck Adams, used to play linebacker for our high school football team."

"Yeah? Stockton doesn't strike me as the football type."

"More like baseball," Marlou said. "Heck used to play that, too. First base."

Where, Nudger thought, he hadn't yet reached. He said, "Stockton told me some unflattering things about Vanita. I don't like to ask you this, Marlou, but is there any truth to them?"

She gave him the Dee look. He wondered if it could bend spoons.

"I mean, to any small degree," Nudger said. "It's important I know. Your sister paid me, and it's my responsibility to clear her name on this, as well as to save both our necks if her killers decide one of us has the diamonds."

"I told you, I never had anything to do with Vanita's private life."

"But what did you know about it?"

Marlou gnawed on her lower lip a while. Then she put her fists on her scrawny hips and stood defiantly. "Vanita liked men, is all. 'Specially that Rupert Winslow. But all men, it seemed."

"Would it be accurate to say she slept around?"

"Well, maybe. I don't know."

"How about drugs?"

"Drugs?"

"She use anything? Carry any kind of habit?"

"Not so far's I know. Men, Mr. Nudger. That was probably her only habit she couldn't seem to quit."

She's quit now, Nudger thought, but didn't say it. What he did say was, "How about telling lies? Did Vanita stretch the truth from time to time?"

"A tad, maybe."

"Marlou?"

"Well, yeah, she did tend to come up with some wild tales now and again. But mainly for entertainment's sake, I'm sure."

Sisters! Nudger thought. He'd had some bad luck in cases involving sisters. And now this! "Why don't you finish getting dressed, Marlou. I'll go with you to the funeral home if you'd like."

She radiated surprise and gratitude. Looked like an actual glow from inside her. "Would you really? I'd sure appreciate it. This's been a weighty burden to shoulder alone."

"No trouble. It might be interesting to see who shows up. Besides, Vanita was my client."

She touched Nudger's arm, then hurried into the bedroom to change to funeral attire. He watched the neat switch of her Levi's-clad hips. Still felt her touch on his arm.

He couldn't help wondering if more than just a fiery temper ran in Dee blood.

13

Delgado's Funeral Home was on Southwest Avenue in an area of St. Louis known as the Hill. It was a largely Italian part of the city, and Nudger wondered why Marlou had chosen it to take care of arrangements for Vanita's funeral. When she told him someone at police headquarters had recommended it, he understood. A number of St. Louis policemen were of Italian descent, and Delgado's had been the scene of more than a few police wakes.

Still, unfairly, Nudger couldn't help thinking Mafia. But there was nothing to suggest Vanita had been connected. Besides, since Jimmy Michaels was blown up in his car several years ago, and the Leisure faction had been decimated by long prison terms, organized crime in St. Louis was minimal.

He parked next to Marlou in the funeral home's blacktop lot and walked inside with her. She was wearing a plain dark-green dress that was a size too large. Black high heels. No jewelry. No makeup, either. That and her lanky frame made her look like a gangly schoolgirl. The gap between her front teeth would make her appear even younger, but she looked as if she'd never smile again.

In the ornate foyer, Nudger told her he saw someone he knew, and she nodded, then started alone toward the room where Vanita was laid out. He touched her arm and offered to go in with her, but she assured him she was fine and didn't need him. Her walk slowed, but she moved with a steady determination. Gritty and practical country girl getting done what was necessary. The way it must have been when she'd identified her sister's body.

Nudger crossed the plush blue carpet to where a large man in a gray suit, standing with his head bowed and his hands folded across his stomach paunch, was staring into the round pool of an indoor fountain. He walked right up next to the man, who hadn't moved a muscle or looked in his direction. But Nudger knew his approach had been noted. He stood quietly beside the man and gazed down at the goldfish swimming lazily in the fountain pond. Waited a while, then said, "Hi, Joe. Somebody you know pass away?"

The fountain, comprised of several stone lily pads and cherubs, made a soothing, repetitive gurgling sound.

Detective Sergeant Joe Martini said, "That a rhetorical question, Nudger, or you want an answer?"

"Rhetorical."

Martini nodded toward the fish. "Don't they make you wish you was on a riverbank somewhere, doing some serious fly casting?"

"Make me think about stuffed flounder," Nudger said.

"Why?"

"Long story."

"Don't tell me, then." Martini turned and looked directly at Nudger. He had a beefy face with gentle brown eyes. Black hair going gray. A semicircular scar on his left cheek that Nudger knew had been made by a broken beer bottle during a peace-disturbance call to a tavern brawl ten years ago. "Saw you walk in with Vanita Lane's sister, Nudger."

"Yeah. The deceased was my client."

Martini chuckled. "Remind me never to hire you."

Nudger knew Martini was here on the "Weep Detail." It was standard procedure for a cop to attend a murder victim's funeral. Killers are unpredictable in a lot of ways, and it wouldn't be the first time one had attended the wake or funeral of the victim. Martini was carefully observing everyone who came into the funeral home and then veered left toward where Vanita Lane was laid out for viewing by mourners. Nudger said, "Anybody interesting been here?"

"Nope. Couple of small-timers. She had some yukky friends, seems to me."

"Such as Rupert Winslow."

"You got that right," Martini said. "Ropes. What an asshole. He was small-time all the way. Fucked up everything he tried."

"She loved him, though."

"Ain't only opposites attract. Or maybe she was the one made him like he was. Then he caused her to be mixed up in something got her killed. Karma, huh? Or poetic justice or some such thing."

"You're being awful hard on her. She's not up for sainthood."

"None of us are likely to be remembered as saints," Martini said. "Mother Teresa excepted, but I don't look for her to drop by tonight."

"You never can tell."

"She's not in town."

"Do me a favor," Nudger said. "If anybody who strikes your interest turns up here, let me know."

"I'll let Hammersmith know. He can tell you. Gotta cover my ass, Nudger."

"Sure. Everybody does except Mother Teresa."

Martini cleared his throat softly. "Now if you don't mind . . ."

Nudger knew what he meant. Martini was trying to be as invisible as possible, and it didn't help to have Nudger standing next to him watching the goldfish. Nudger drifted away toward where Vanita was laid out.

Delgado's had done a good job. She was beautiful in a casket lined with white tufted satin. Only the upper half of her body was visible. Nudger tried not to think of the damage beneath the blue dress, the carnage in the motel cottage. Her ruined hands were encased in flesh-colored Latex gloves. Looked almost normal. Her eyes were closed lightly. Her lips were barely pressed together.

While Nudger stood there, a couple of guys in suits even cheaper than the ones in his closet came up and paused by the other side of the casket. One of them whispered, "Jesus! She looks just like she did when she was alive." The other said, "Yeah. On her back, and she might open her mouth and spout bullshit any second." Neither man changed expression during this exchange. They walked toward a small knot of mourners near a grouping of baroque furniture.

Nudger walked over to where Marlou was standing alone near a colorful floral arrangement. Other than the arrangement, there were three wreaths. He glanced at a card and saw that the flowers were from Marlou. When she saw him she tried a smile. She was almost as pale as her sister.

He said, "You know any of these people?"

"Not really. Know who a couple of them are. That man over there told me he works for the lounge where Vanita used to be a waitress. Those two guys that were next to you up near the casket are from there, too. That woman, the one with, like, the wide-brimmed hat, ran this other place where Vanita worked some years ago."

"Other place?"

"Not the lounge, I mean."

"What kinda place?"

"Massage parlor, I think it was. That was when she was real young, though. Even before the lucky day she met Rupert." For a second it looked as if Marlou might crack and begin to sob. But she sucked in a deep breath and composed herself. "Wish to God she was still working there and never met the bastard."

"I wish it with you," Nudger said. He glanced around. "You gonna be okay here?"

"Sure. I'll do what needs doing. That's the way I always been."

Nudger didn't doubt it. He rested his fingertips on the back of her hand. "I'll talk to you tomorrow."

She stared at him. "Thanks for your help, Mr. Nudger. Listen, though, one thing I wanna keep straight is . . . well, I ain't rich. I mean, I never hired you to discover who killed Vanita, though God knows I'd like to find out. I can't afford a private investigator."

Nudger touched her cool hand again. It reminded him of Vanita's gloved hands folded across her chest. Vanita's hands at peace, beyond all feeling, all pain. *A massage parlor.* "I'm still working for your sister," he said. "And for myself."

She breathed out loudly and nodded, smiling in a way that made him feel like gulping. Ran her tongue around the space between her teeth and then clamped her lips together. For a moment she looked too much like her sister in the coffin.

Nudger muttered, "Sorry about Vanita," and walked away, pretending she probably hadn't noticed the tightness in his voice.

Martini was still standing idly near the indoor fountain, but Nudger only glanced at him while walking past. The plainclothes cop stared harder at the goldfish. If Martini was on watch in here, there was no doubt another cop was keeping an eye on whoever might simply hang around the outside of the funeral home. That made Nudger feel more secure. The police might not be the only ones who used Delgado's as a place to make connections with those who'd been involved with Vanita Lane or Rupert Winslow.

Nudger thought it unlikely that anyone would follow him home from the funeral parlor.

And he was right; no one did follow.

They were waiting for him in his living room when he walked into his apartment.

14

One was standing near the window. The other was perched on the arm of Nudger's sofa and had his arms crossed. Both men looked at Nudger when he entered. They smiled. The one by the window was in his thirties, handsome, but with a face almost too pretty beneath a head of full, wavy black hair. He was on the short side, but he had a lean waist and wide, powerful shoulders, a deep chest. All-American quarterback type, but way too small for the pros. He was dressed all-American, too; navy blue blazer, gray slacks, red-and-white striped tie. Might have been a Republican fund-raiser.

The other man was older, maybe in his fifties. He was dressed like a pool hustler who'd just worked a con. Had on black slacks and a gray-and-black-checked sport coat that had so much silk in it the gray took on a silvery glitter. White shirt open at the neck to allow a peek at a gold chain. He was so thin he was almost skeletal, causing the coat to drape crookedly from his shoulders as if it were on a bent hanger. His face was long, with equine features. Bulging brown eyes. Oversized yellow teeth. He had a yellowish complexion to go with the teeth.

He looked sick. "Ah, Mr. Nudger!" he said, as if they'd been waiting a while and here Nudger was at last.

On the floor, directly between the two men, was a small square metal bird cage with a yellow canary in it. The sort of outfit you might buy in a dime store on a whim for somebody else's kid. The canary wasn't singing, just sitting on a wooden perch and fluffing its feathers. It was probably wondering what the hell was going on. Like Nudger.

The handsome man by the window was still smiling like a toothpaste ad sprung to life.

Nudger said, "And you two are . . . ?"

"Here to see you," the skeleton said. He uncrossed his arms and slid the long, yellow fingers of his right hand into a pocket of the silky sport coat, striking an exaggerated genteel casualness that rang about as true as a wooden bell. He wheezed slightly with each breath, as if he were functioning at high altitude and was unused to it. His bulbous eyes fixed hard, almost fanatically, on Nudger, and he said, "Why don't you c'mon in and sit down in that chair?" It was more than a suggestion; maybe there was a gun in that sport coat pocket. Maybe not.

Maybe was enough. Nudger crossed the living room slowly and sat down in the wing chair that faced the sofa at an angle. The skeleton watched him carefully, working his tongue around inside his cheek as if something might be stuck between his molars. All-American was gazing out the window again.

Nudger said, "So what's this about?" Though he had a pretty good idea what.

"Diamonds," said the man staring out the window. "About diamonds."

Nudger said, "I'm a cubic zirconia man, myself."

"I can see that." The man didn't turn from the window.

"Actually," the skeleton said, "we came here to ask what the late Miss Vanita Lane might have told you about these diamonds."

"*These* diamonds? *What* diamonds?"

Skeleton smiled with his horsey choppers. His narrow face

creased like old parchment. He wheezed. "We think Miss Lane knew the whereabouts of some diamonds that belong to us."

"The late Miss Lane."

"Ah, yeah. I suppose that bears repeating. We think she mighta told you where the diamonds are. That only leaves you to tell us."

Nudger knew who these two were, even if they wouldn't give their names: the diamond thieves who'd fallen out with Rupert Winslow and then murdered him. The men who'd tortured and killed Vanita. Fear was threatening to turn his joints rubbery, cause him to lose control. He fought against that. Knew his survival might depend on using the old gray matter. Figured, why not the truth? "She thought the diamonds were on the plane."

Both men stared solemnly at Nudger and said nothing.

"The one that blew up at the airport."

All-American said, "An explosion wouldn't destroy diamonds. They're the hardest things in the world. Except maybe for us."

"Vanita didn't realize that."

The skeleton shook his head sadly. "That I don't buy. Woman like Vanita, she knew diamonds."

"But not where these diamonds are," Nudger said.

"She hire you to find them?"

"That's right." Nudger didn't think it wise to reveal she'd actually hired him to protect her from the two men standing and staring down at him.

"So how you been doing?" the skeleton asked. "Got any ideas?"

"I don't think there ever were any diamonds. What I found out was that Vanita Lane had an overactive imagination and a reputation for stretching the truth."

All-American smiled. "Overactive this, overactive that."

"Ah, she had her problems," said the skeleton.

"She was a devious, lying cunt," All-American said softly.

"True," the skeleton agreed, "but let's not speak other than kindly of the dead."

Nudger remembered Vanita's broken fingers. The flesh-colored gloves on her hands in the funeral home. "If she'd known where the diamonds were, she'd have told you."

"You'd think that, all right." *Wheeze. Wheeze.* "I mean even when we . . . Anyway, she really might not know where they are. What Rupert Winslow really did with them."

"We can't be absolutely sure, though," said All-American.

The skeleton grinned wider. A death's-head. "That's true. Because Miss Lane had her aforementioned character flaws, and she was one tough little bitch."

"Had steel balls," All-American said. "In a manner of speaking."

"She'd have told you," Nudger said. He didn't want to say too much about the torture-murder. Didn't want to prompt a repeat performance right here in the apartment. But why else were these two here? Fear tried to claw its way up his throat. He swallowed. Absently touched his violently working stomach.

"Got some kinda problem?" asked the skeleton.

"Nervous stomach."

"Tough shit, in your business. Must get in the way of the job."

"From time to time."

"Thing is," the skeleton said, "Miss Lane was gutsy enough we just can't be sure if she was telling the truth at that motel, even under the painful circumstances. She mighta went down lying her ass off."

"Wouldn't of been the first time," said the one by the window. Speaking unkindly of the dead again. Nudger decided to let it pass.

The skeleton gave a brittle kind of chuckle and shook his head. "Last thing she did, Nudger, she spit on my friend here. Believe that? Spit right in his face just before he . . . Well, point is, the lady had some intestinal fortitude. We were plenty impressed."

"Balls of steel, all right," said the other one. "What about you, Nudger? You got them kinda balls?"

"Mine are more balsa wood, but I don't know any more than I'm telling you."

The skeleton nodded, wise as Death. "Could be. We're not here to pull your strings, 'cause you probably wouldn't tell us shit anyway. Though I doubt you'd do any spitting there toward the last."

He nodded again, this time in the direction of All-American, who reached down and opened the bird cage, stuck in his arm, and removed the canary. He cupped it gently in his right hand and stroked it softly on the head, as if trying to coax a tweet out of it.

The skeleton said, "Like birds, Nudger?"

"Sure." *Not pigeons.*

All-American walked over to stand near Nudger's chair. He held the canary out so Nudger had a good view of it.

Squeezed.

The canary's beak gaped wide but no sound came out. Its head thrashed. A leg found its way twiglike between All-American's fingers and flailed in desperation. All-American grinned and kept squeezing. Something began to emerge from the canary's beak. Nudger's stomach was spinning and he felt light-headed. Couldn't look away. Heard himself say, "Ah, Jesus, stop!"

All-American said, "Okay," and dropped what was left of the canary on the floor at Nudger's feet. Laughed and said, "Teach it to sing, why don't you?"

Only raw fear kept Nudger from leaping up and hitting the man. But then, that was the idea.

The skeleton said, "Keep doing what you been doing, Nudger. Looking for the diamonds. Only now *we're* your clients. That clear?"

"Clear." Nudger couldn't look at the bird.

The skeleton slouched toward the door. All-American followed, wiping his hands on a handkerchief. As if he'd been doing minor work on his car, got some grease on his fingers.

All-American held the door open for the skeleton, and both men stepped out into the hall. The skeleton stuck his head back inside, though. "We'll be in touch for your progress reports. Now go ahead and clean up that thing that used to be a bird. And remember while you're doing it, you got any ideas about not telling us what you learn, and we'll make you sing even if that canary didn't."

Nudger sat and listened to them tromp down the hall. They were joking to each other about something even before they reached the steps, laughing loudly in the echoing stairwell. About what? Vanita! The crushed canary? About Nudger?

Probably it didn't make much difference to them.

Nudger could no longer hear the two men.

Reluctantly, he stared down at the dead bird. Saw Vanita. *Oh, God!*

He got a wad of paper towels from the kitchen and cleaned up the mess, even though doing so wrung out his insides.

Story of his life.

15

Nudger climbed out of bed at nine the next morning, and after a stop at the office and doughnut shop, he drove toward the Third District station to see Hammersmith. For Nudger, nine o'clock was oversleeping. His body felt stiff and his head throbbed as if someone were drilling on the front of his skull from the inside. The sun beating through the windshield made him sneeze. Which made his eyes water. Which made his nose run. *Sniff! Sniff!* God, this was agony!

He took a sip of Danny's coffee from the Styrofoam cup in his right hand, steering with his left. The cup had a plastic lid with a tiny triangular drink-hole, but still some of the hot liquid dribbled down his chin. He didn't care. If the sneeze had been a warning of a summer cold, Danny's coffee would smite any lesser germ in his system.

Nudger felt a little better by the time he reached the station house. Headache almost gone.

He parked in a visitor's slot and walked across the lot toward the side entrance. Saw Hammersmith's unmarked Pontiac parked in the shade. Someone had traced LEGALIZE MARIJUANA in the dust on the driver-side door. Maybe Hammersmith himself had done it to tweak the cops in Narcotics; sometimes he displayed a devilish sense of humor.

Hammersmith had been at work for more than two hours. Nudger had called last night and was expected, but still the obese lieutenant looked surprised when Nudger gave a perfunctory knock and walked into his office. He'd thought Nudger would arrive at eight. "What's this, Nudge? You wander into Springer's office by mistake before you found your way here?"

"Overslept."

"Oh? Home Shopping Network keep you up?"

"No," Nudger said, "it was fear, not herringbone gold chains."

Hammersmith rubbed a smooth, fleshy jowl. One of his pink and pudgy hands floated up from the desk and motioned for Nudger to sit down. Nudger sat in the uncomfortable straight-backed chair in front of the desk. There was a stack of report forms on the desk, transcribed by a clerk from the handwritten accounts of patrolmen.

"These guys," Hammersmith said, tapping the reports with a cellophane-wrapped cigar, "they still write about subjects having blond hair and eyes. And arms and legs getting decapitated."

"Some things never change," Nudger said. "You don't have to be a literary giant to be a good cop."

"Thank God. Norman Mailers we ain't got." He propped the still-wrapped cigar against the ashtray on the desk corner, positioning it carefully so it was aimed at Nudger like a missile moments away from launching. Nudger knew his time in the office was limited. Crime was an ongoing condition and Hammersmith was busy. Hammersmith made a graceful fat man's gesture with his right hand, as if to signify that Nudger had center stage and his full attention. "So let's hear your story, Nudge."

Nudger told it.

Hammersmith sat there like Buddha taking it easy and listened, staring at a point high on the opposite wall until Nudger was finished. Nothing on his broad, smooth features indicated any sort of reaction.

Finally he lowered his eyes to look at Nudger and said, "Think the two guys followed you home from the funeral parlor?"

Nudger knew what Hammersmith was thinking. Had to disappoint him. "My impression was they'd been waiting for me a while. You might check with Martini, but I'd bet he didn't see these two."

"Ah, you noticed Martini at the funeral home."

"Only because I know him," Nudger said. "Otherwise I'd have thought he was just another mourner seeking solace in goldfish."

"Whazzat?" Hammersmith made a move as if to reach for the cigar. He wouldn't take much lip from Nudger today.

"Just an expression," Nudger said.

Hammersmith said, "Your description of the two badmen in your apartment doesn't strike a chord."

"I'm not surprised. They figure to be diamond thieves from New York. And they say they're the ones who killed Vanita Lane."

"I hope you get a chance to mention that in court." Hammersmith levitated his great weight from his chair and said, "Wait a minute, Nudge." Coasted from the office with his peculiar bulky grace. As if Mikhail Barishnikov had gained fifty pounds and joined the department.

Hammersmith returned five minutes later with a set of mug books and a long, green-and-white, fan-fold computer printout. "Computer tells us the names on this list have East Coast connections. Wanna check on them here in the office or in one of the interrogation rooms?"

"Be more comfortable in a room," Nudger said. "Less bother, too."

"For sure, Nudge."

Hammersmith led him down the hall to a small institutional-green room. It had a single wire-reinforced window and an overhead light fixture encased in what looked like a small metal cage. Reminded Nudger of the bird cage last night in his apartment. Made his stomach lurch.

"Lemme know when you finish with those," Hammersmith said. "We need to, we'll get you some more."

He closed the door and left Nudger alone.

The only furniture in the room was a rectangular oak table, old and scarred. Darkened at the edges from desperate sweat. Two mismatched, sturdy oak chairs. Nudger looked around at the bare walls and tiny dust-coated window, grateful he wasn't claustrophobic.

He chose the more comfortable-looking of the two chairs and sat down. Consulted the computer printout, then opened the first mug book and scanned it page by page as if it were a family photo album.

It wasn't until the third set of books that he flipped a page and saw the younger but unmistakable features of the man who'd crushed the canary. The man's name and some vital statistics were listed, along with an arrest record: Roger Bobinet, A.K.A. Bobby Rogers, A.K.A. Roger Bing. He'd been thirty-two years old at the time of his arrest for car theft. Made him thirty-six now. He was 5'8", 185 pounds, said the book. Hair black, eyes blue. No distinguishing marks. His mug shots looked like publicity photos for a confident, aspiring young actor. As if the prison garb and the number across his chest were props on a clean-cut straight arrow playing the Humphrey Bogart bad-ass role in a college production of *Petrified Forest*. Not even his eyes gave him away. Few mothers would object to the handsome Bobinet showing up at the door to escort their daughters.

Some of those mothers might not see their daughters again.

Nudger kept the heavy mug book open to the telltale page and carried it toward Hammersmith's office. A cop he knew, leading a handcuffed suspect down the hall toward the holdover cells, nodded to him. The suspect, a shirtless, muscular black man, kept repeating, "No justice, no fuckin' justice 'less you got money for some hightone lawyer . . ." The man was dragging his feet like a kid not wanting to get to school. There might be something to what he said, Nudger thought.

Hammersmith was on the phone. He made a face at Nudger, who sat down again in the chair by the desk, the mug book open in his lap. Then Hammersmith ignored Nudger and stared fixedly at the ceiling as if there were an escape hatch up there he might want to use. He said "Yes. Yes. Yes" into the phone. Said "No. No. No" and then hung up without saying good-bye. Couldn't have been Headquarters.

Nudger said, "Found one." He leaned forward and laid the open mug book on Hammersmith's desk, then touched a fingertip to Roger Bobinet's profile shot.

Hammersmith propped his fleshy chin on a fist and stared down at the photo Nudger touched. "Looks like one of my teenage son's friends."

"He's thirty-two there," Nudger pointed out.

"Could be nineteen or thirty-nine. One of those faces, huh? Like Johnny Carson a few years ago."

Nudger saw no resemblance between Carson and Bobinet but said nothing. The cigar was still propped like a Minuteman missile against the ashtray.

"What we'll do," Hammersmith said, "is run this through NCIC." He stood up, lifted the mug book still open, and cradled it in a pudgy arm. "Only take a minute. Miracle of the microchip." NCIC was the FBI's National Crime Information Center, a kind of computer data base of criminality. The main computer at FBI headquarters contained approximately twenty million records of wanted or missing people, stolen property, and criminal histories. It had been set up over twenty years ago and had proved itself useful.

Nudger said he didn't mind waiting. The odds were good that if Bobinet was in the St. Louis records for auto theft, the FBI would have a sheet on him.

Hammersmith returned in less time than it had taken him to get the first set of mug books, another green-and-white computer printout flapping in his right hand.

He was smiling almost sadly, in a way Nudger didn't like.

"This Bobinet is some pumpkin," he said. He settled down behind his desk and scanned the printout. "Did time in New Jersey for rape when he was sixteen. At nineteen a stretch in New York for burglary and assault with a deadly weapon—a crossbow, of all things. Then he grew up. Put his childish toys behind him, as it says in the Bible. Or something like that. Arrest but no conviction for the torture killing of a barmaid in Newark. There's a warrant out for him now for the abduction and murder of a twelve-year-old girl in New York." Hammersmith dropped the printout on his desk. "Bobinet's not one of the white hats, Nudge. Best you be careful."

"Caution's my middle name."

"You got a string of names, and 'Dumb' is in there somewhere."

"Thanks."

"Well, let's make it 'Stubborn' instead of 'Dumb.' But sometimes that amounts to the same thing. 'Dead,' it can be, in this case."

Nudger knew Hammersmith was right. Though he preferred "Persistent" instead of "Stubborn."

Hammersmith said, "Guys like this Bobinet, so normal on the outside, but with this sorta sheet, are the most dangerous kinda psychos. They're like members of another species that's learned to adapt but never become really human. He might kill you casual as a farmer doing in a chicken, only he'd probably take longer and enjoy it."

Nudger didn't like thinking of himself as sacrificial poultry, but he got Hammersmith's point. "How long ago'd he kill the kid in New York?"

"Allegedly," Hammersmith reminded Nudger.

"Okay. Bobinet or somebody else."

Hammersmith squinted down at the printout. "That was . . . hmm, eighteen months ago. I got a list of Bobinet's known associates, too. Had the computer do a cross-check. None of them fits the ID of this guy you said looked like a skeleton."

"He could have changed," Nudger said. "Might be sick.

Even his features wouldn't look the same with a lot of weight loss from illness."

"Possibly. I'll request photos from NCIC. It'll give me a chance to use the fax machine." Hammersmith leaned back and finally unwrapped the cigar. He got out his silver lighter with the blowtorch flame. Fired up the cigar and grinned around it. Conversation over.

Nudger held his breath until he'd stood up and gotten his nose where the air was still unfouled by green smoke. He said, "Thanks for your help, Jack."

"Nothing, Nudge." Hammersmith rested the cigar in the ashtray. Smoke uncoiled from it like a charmed cobra. Probably just as deadly. "This Bobinet and the other guy'll no doubt contact you by phone. Let me know when that happens."

"Why don't I set up a meeting with them? You can be there and make the collar."

"That's a laugh. They'll never agree to a meeting. You'll see them next unexpectedly—when they choose."

"Wanna put a tap on my phone?"

"It wouldn't be worth the trouble. Old hands like the people you're mixed up with'll use a public phone and not stay on it long."

The thick curl of smoke from the cigar seemed to notice Nudger and twisted toward him with malice. He backed toward the door.

"I'll let you know when they call me," he said.

"If they *do* contact you in person, Nudge, be sure and let me know that, too, soon as they leave. If you can."

Nudger swallowed; his stomach was convulsing. He wasn't sure if it was fear or the cigar smoke.

As he was walking out the door he heard Hammersmith say, "Teach you to hand your card to strange women."

16

The phone was jangling when Nudger walked into his office. He lifted the receiver, then stretched the cord and his left arm so he could switch on the air conditioner. It made its irritating *pinka! pinka! pinka!* noise until he slapped it.

"Mr. Nudger?"

He recognized the soft country drawl of Marlou Dee. Told her he was indeed Mr. Nudger, but just Nudger would do.

"You ain't got a first name?"

"I do, but I don't like it."

"Okay, Nudger. What I called about is, I think somebody's, like, been in my apartment."

"What makes you think so?"

"Well, things ain't quite like they was when I went out this morning for about an hour to get some groceries. I mean, it ain't like the place is a mess, or that anything's actually missing or even been moved. Well, stuff's been moved, I'm sure, but, like, hardly more'n a few inches here and there. Sometimes less'n that. Even my spices in the kitchen drawer ain't quite in the same order. The turmeric is shoved way near the back. Sage is where the turmeric used to be."

A neighbor out to steal fennel seed, Nudger thought. "Check the silverware?" he asked, realizing he wasn't taking this as seriously as he should. Maybe because it figured Marlou would be a bit paranoid after the run-in with Edward Franks yesterday. Who wouldn't be?

"Got mostly cheap metal knives an' forks I filched from Steak 'n' Shake restaurants, Mr. Nudger. Nobody'd steal that stuff. What I'm talking about's not just in the kitchen, though. Like, in the living room the sofa cushions are sorta cattywampus, like they been taken off and shoved back on in a hurry and not been sat on since. And the coffee table's at a funny angle."

Nudger was reminded of the comedian who claimed that everything in his apartment had been stolen and then replaced by an exact duplicate. Only there was nothing funny about this. It was possible the skeleton and Bobinet had learned Vanita had a sister. It was also possible Nudger had led them to Marlou. Nudger the kiss of death. He shivered.

Said, "I'll drive over and have a look at things."

" 'Preciate that, Nudger. I guess I'm a little skittish lately." She sounded apologetic. Sorry to be putting him out even in the slightest.

"I'm skittish lately, too," Nudger told her. "It's going around like flu. See you in about half an hour."

She opened the door before he had a chance to knock. Wearing a halter top and Levi's today. Levi's seemed to be her basic uniform when she wasn't at funeral homes. This pair was threadbare and faded and incredibly tight; he imagined she had to lie down and squirm into them inch by inch in order to pack them with Marlou. He pushed away the image that formed in his mind. Her halter top was a vibrant aquamarine and made of some sort of elastic material that clung to her nublike breasts. The ridges of her ribs were visible through the material when she twisted her torso. She was one of those women who'd be built like a teenager until menopause.

She smiled with her gapped front teeth and stepped back to give him room to enter. As he moved past her he caught a mingled scent of perfume and perspiration that was oddly appealing.

The old window air conditioner was flailing away at the heat and not doing a bad job; the apartment was cool. Nudger wasn't sure how long that would last; condensation on the unit's plastic grill was already forming a blanket of ice that would stifle air flow.

Marlou noticed him looking at the air conditioner and said, "I gotta turn it off every other hour or it freezes up and gets useless as tits on a boar hog. Landlord's been s'pose to fix it. Till then I'm cool half the time."

Nudger said, "I'm glad I got here during one of the *on* hours."

"Fifty-fifty's better odds than on most things in life."

"Wise girl." He walked slowly around the living room, then went into the kitchen, where Marlou showed him how things in the drawers and cabinets had been slightly rearranged. Tiny spice bottles and boxes shuffled around. Whoever had been here knew nothing of spices. Had no sense of thyme. She closed the spice drawer, stirring a pungent whiff of air that almost made Nudger sneeze. "Even the mayonnaise was, like, shoved way to the back of the refrigerator," she said. "I never keep it back there. Use it all the time for sandwiches."

"Never ketchup or mustard?"

"Not on sandwiches. In some ways I'm a finicky eater."

"What about your bedroom?"

"Stuff in my closet and dresser drawers looks like it mighta been gone through, too. Wanna look?"

"No, I'll take your word for it." Nudger had already decided she was right; the apartment did show unmistakable indication it had been searched by people who knew what they were doing. But despite TV shows and crime novels to the contrary, no one could conduct a really thorough search and not leave some signs that would be noted by whoever lived on the premises.

Especially if that person was a nervous and observant young woman who used only mayonnaise on her sandwiches.

"So watcha think, Nudger?"

"The place has been tossed?"

"Searched, you mean?"

"Yep."

"For those diamonds, I guess. That Mr. Franks, you figure?"

"I hope so, but I doubt it."

"The police?"

"Not likely."

"Who, then?"

"Somebody you don't know. And I don't want you to meet them."

Her naive green eyes got wide, but she seemed more intrigued than scared. "The diamond thieves, huh?"

He nodded. "The same men who killed Vanita."

On target. She looked scared now. Her lips tightened over her protruding teeth and her Adam's apple danced. "God, they was right here in my apartment." She glanced around as if someone might still be here, hiding and waiting for the chance to get her alone. Not impossible at that. Nudger's stomach stirred.

"What are your plans for the day?" he asked.

"I gotta work someplace from noon till five, then I was gonna go stay at the funeral home till it closed."

"Where do you work?"

"I don't have a regular job. I'm filling in a couple of weeks for a receptionist at a realty company."

"Can they get someone to take your place?"

"Today, you mean?"

"For an indefinite period, starting tomorrow."

"I s'pose they could if I asked. I was gonna be off tomorrow anyway, for Vanita's funeral."

"I'll drive you to work," Nudger said, "then pick you up at five. I'm gonna stay close to you, spend the night here on the sofa. Then I think you better leave town. Be unavailable for a while."

"Hide out, you mean? Like Vanita was doing?"

"Not like Vanita," Nudger said quickly. More than a little defensively. "Out of town where you won't be found. Vanita said she and you were from southwest Missouri, so I plan to put you up someplace northeast. Far away, but not so far that I can't get to you by car in a few hours. Say, Hannibal."

"Mr. Nudger, I can't afford—"

"I'll pay. Your sister gave me a retainer."

She gnawed on her lower lip and looked as if she were trying to make up her mind. Breathing hard beneath the halter.

"There isn't much choice, Marlou. Remember what happened to Vanita."

"Can't forget it."

"No, I guess you can't."

"But, like, why would those men think *I* got the diamonds?"

"You're Vanita's sister. They probably only suspect you know something about the diamonds, but that's enough for them because they've got nothing else to go on."

"Heck! I betcha them diamonds never left New York."

"You're probably right. But the way they figure it, Rupert Winslow could have mailed them to Vanita, and she might have given them to you for safekeeping or told you where she'd hidden them."

Marlou glanced around bitterly at her meager possessions. "Hah! Me with a million dollars in diamonds. Ain't it a weird thought?"

"One we all think from time to time," Nudger said. "But the men who killed Vanita are thinking it all the time, and they'll do anything to make it come true."

She sighed. "I s'pose you're right."

"It's eleven-fifteen," Nudger said. "When do you want to leave for work?"

"I was gonna have some lunch afore I go. Wanna join me? Be just a sandwich and soda, but everything's fresh from the store."

"Sure," Nudger said. "Sounds good."

He went with her into the kitchen and sat at the small,

white-enameled wood table while she gathered ingredients for lunch. It was warmer in there; the cool air from the laboring window unit barely made it through the doorway. A strand of Marlou's red hair flopped down and lay plastered by perspiration to her glistening forehead. She moved lightly and quickly, lost in her task. Knew what she was doing. Hardscrabble Ozark girl who liked to work in the kitchen.

They had Diet Pepsi, potato chips, sweet pickles, and bologna sandwiches with tomato slices and lettuce on them. And mayonnaise.

17

Marlou changed into black slacks and a matching blazer. Wore a white blouse with what looked like a man's silk bow tie. Didn't look at all like a man.

Nudger drove her in her businesswoman's outfit to Fisk Realty on South Kingshighway and watched her push open the glass front door and sashay inside. She wobbled slightly, as if unused to wearing high heels. He imagined she usually went barefoot alone in her apartment.

From where Nudger was parked across the street, he could see her talking to a fat man in a light-colored suit. Then she sat down behind the receptionist desk, and her abbreviated workday began. Within a minute or two Nudger saw her pick up a phone, swivel her head and call to someone in the office.

The office had to be small. It was at the end of a low, one-story building and was flanked on the north side by a florist. Nudger wondered if the flowers at the funeral home had come from the florist; convenient for Marlou. Maybe the only thing convenient in her life lately.

Nudger sat and kept an eye on her for a while, though he

figured she was relatively safe in the tiny, bustling office and in plain view from the street.

After about half an hour he drove around the block slowly, then checked Fisk Realty again. He did that now and then for the next couple of hours, parking from time to time on side streets, choosing different routes so he wouldn't attract attention. Kingshighway was a major thoroughfare; it was easy to drive past Fisk Realty frequently without being noticeable. Occasionally customers would come and go, and more sharply dressed people, usually carrying briefcases or attaché cases, entered or left the office. Salespeople, probably. They had the look.

Marlou continued to sit primly behind her desk, womaning the phones. Frequently someone would be standing nearby talking to her or receiving written messages. She was working more or less steadily, but time had to be crawling for her. It was for Nudger.

After a while his stomach growled something like "Eeeeen-ough!" and he started the Granada and headed north to Uncle Bill's Pancake House.

Uncle Bill's was a South St. Louis institution that served the best pancakes in the universe. Nudger had a stack of them and some black coffee for supper. Then he sat for a while in the booth and watched traffic stream past on Kingshighway. The afternoon was finally giving way to early evening, but it was still ovenlike beyond the tinted window and slanted awning. Sun glinted off passing windshields and the rows of polished used cars at the dealer's lot across the street. CREAM PUFF, proclaimed a sign in one of the cars' windshields. Talking about me? Nudger wondered, remembering his stomach's violent reaction to what Roger Bobinet had done to the canary. It was, after all, merely a dead bird.

No, it was more than that, he knew; it was what the dead bird meant. How close in reality it was to what might happen to Nudger himself, and in the same dispassionate manner. He was sure the life of an animal and the life of a human being were of equal value to Bobinet. That was how he could do to a fellow human what had been done to Vanita. That was what had chilled Nudger's blood when he'd witnessed the crushing of the canary. Roger Bobinet's tactics were primal and savage, but they worked as surely as heads of the enemy stacked near an ancient city gate. They instilled terror, and it stuck.

After five cups of coffee, Nudger couldn't stand the bitter taste in his mouth, and his inactivity. It was possible he'd become one with the booth; affixed there like some sea creature to a reef.

He took a sip of water, left a generous tip for tying up the booth for so long, and paid the cashier. He pushed through the door near the register, passing the ornate ceramic display in the foyer, wondering who would buy the silver wall clock fashioned to look like a toilet seat. Beneath the toilet seat clock was an equally garish statuette of Christ laboring beneath his cross on the road to the crucifixion. The Christ statue was equipped with a switch and was actually a lamp. Ah, South St. Louis.

Nudger hovered around Fisk Realty until quarter to five, then parked a few hundred feet down the block and waited for Marlou.

Twenty minutes passed before she emerged from the realty office, looking as fresh as when she'd entered. Youth. Even the dreariness of routine couldn't grind it down. Look at the spring in her legs. She was probably ready to dance.

"What'd you do while I was working?" she asked, sliding into the car and slamming the door hard enough to make the rearview mirror slip out of kilter.

"Oh, I hung around, had a bite to eat." He straightened the mirror, checking the street behind them. Nothing unusual there.

"Eat," she said. "That sure enough sounds good. Yakking on the phone works up a powerful appetite."

Nudger had never noticed that, but then he wasn't one to hang on the phone like Gidget.

"There's, like, a great place near here," Marlou said. "Uncle Bill's."

Ten minutes later Nudger found himself in the same booth, sipping even more coffee and watching Marlou devour a large order of buckwheat pancakes and bacon. "I pig out here regular," she mumbled around a mouthful of hotcake. Would she reach age forty and two hundred pounds simultaneously? He couldn't imagine her at either of those figures.

After dinner he drove her back to her apartment and waited while she changed into her mourning clothes. She still wore the black blazer, but now with a dark blouse and gray skirt. In the living room she said she hadn't had much experience with death and dying, and she struck a kind of Sears-catalog-model pose and asked in a serious voice if she looked okay. He said sure, she looked fine. Then he went with her to the funeral home.

No one came to view Vanita tonight, and Nudger didn't look into the still-open casket near the front of the room. Even Martini wasn't there. Nudger sat outside the room and leafed through the morning paper, now and then glancing in at Marlou. She was seated on a small brocade ivory sofa with her legs crossed, looking young and lonely. Made his heart ache. Also his stomach. He treated himself to his last antacid tablet and dropped the crumpled silver foil into an ashtray.

He remained at the edge of the Resurrection Cemetery during the funeral the next morning. Leaning against an ancient sycamore tree while a blue jay on a low branch kept cocking its head and natterering at him. Nudger wasn't about to move out of the shade. Let the bird bitch.

He wanted to stay close to Marlou, but the less he was actually seen with her the better. The pallbearers were furnished by the funeral home, as was the minister. It figured Vanita hadn't been a churchgoer. The only mourner other than Marlou was the woman she'd told him had been Vanita's boss at a lounge.

The morning was beautiful. The service was brief. About all you can ask of a funeral, other than that it isn't yours.

Afterward Marlou spoke for a while with the minister, who

laid a soft and lingering hand on her shoulder, like a televangelist curing her of all things before walking away to one of the funeral home limos. Vanita's former boss didn't say anything, only glanced at Marlou and then minced away with the peculiar rolling gait of overweight women on high heels, toward the Porsche convertible she'd driven in the short funeral procession.

The funeral home's two black limos and the gleaming hearse glided slowly from the cemetery. The irrepressible sun bounced off them gaily, as if this morning marked a beginning rather than an end.

Marlou stood for a moment staring at Vanita's casket waiting to be lowered into a grave that was for the moment surrounded by what looked like artificial turf that had been peeled from an infield. Then she turned abruptly and walked through sun-dappled sunlight toward Nudger. The broken light made her seem to be moving jerkily, though her stride was smooth.

When she got closer he could see the redness and puffiness of her eyes. She wouldn't look directly at him. She fished in her black purse for a pair of oversized violet-lensed sunglasses, put them on and looked like a kid playing movie star.

All she said as she strode past Nudger toward the Granada was, "Let's get on up to Hannibal."

Until now, she'd seemed somewhat reluctant to go into hiding. Maybe the finality of the funeral had impressed her. The realization that now Vanita was no more than memory.

They went back to Marlou's apartment so she could pack. As soon as they were inside, she slipped off her shoes. Nudger watched her walk into the bedroom, carrying one in each hand.

Then he heard her shriek. Not a scream exactly. More a violent intake of breath, but almost as loud as a scream.

His heart slammed in his chest as he ran toward the bedroom.

Marlou was bent over. Retching. There was vomit splatter on her black shoes, still held in each hand. The shoe in her right hand was dangling by a thin strap between her fingers and looked ready to drop.

At first Nudger didn't understand what was going on. Then he saw the dead animal on the bed. A medium-size brown dog. It was sprawled on its back with its legs askew, as if playing dead. It wasn't playing, though. It had been disemboweled, not neatly. Near the foot of the bed was a small wreath with R.I.P. printed on its silk ribbon. Protocol had been observed; there was a card.

Nudger averted his eyes from the dog and leaned down to read the card. Black felt-tip printing said SORRY ABOUT YOUR SISTER. DEATH CAN HAPPEN ANYWHERE TO ANYONE. He wasn't surprised to see there was no signature.

Marlou retched again. Coughed.

Nudger, floating somewhere above all this, said, "Your dog?" His voice was choked.

Marlou shook her head violently. "Ain't got a dog. Holy God, who'd do this, Nudger?"

"Somebody I know who likes to use the animal world to make his point."

Marlou was standing up straight now, looking better, though she was still pale. She was a country girl and had seen plenty of dead animals, but not like this. On her bed. At the head of the bed, propped on a pillow, was the Raggedy Ann doll, still grinning widely with determined cheer. Nudger wondered if Marlou slept with the doll. Its childish and innocent presence made the butchery seem even worse.

Nudger forced his thoughts into some kind of order. Found some resolve, though he still refused to fully comprehend what had happened here. He was a city boy, and this was simply too horrible.

He clutched Marlou's shoulders and pointed her toward the bathroom. "Get cleaned up," he said. "Then get packed."

Her wide eyes rolled to the butchered dog. "Aw, Christ, Nudger . . ."

He gave her a shove, and she went. Moving like a zombie, but she went.

He swallowed bile. Stumbled into the kitchen. Found a large black plastic trash bag in the cabinet beneath the sink.

He returned to the bedroom and turned off ninety percent of his mind so he could do what had to be done. The smell of blood and corruption was in his mouth now as well as in his nose. It was taste. With his eyes almost closed, he quickly folded the bedspread around the bloody dog. Standing as far back as possible, he lifted the surprisingly heavy bundle and lowered it into the trash bag. Stuffed the funeral wreath in on top of it. He hurried back to the kitchen and got a wire twist, then quickly fastened the top of the bag.

He carried the ghastly bundle out the back door, then down some steps to a door leading to a metal porch and fire escape. After lugging the bag to the alley, he left it behind the garage. He didn't like the way it sloshed when he dropped it.

His own stomach was reacting now. In the back yard, up close to the building, he leaned over and vomited. Spat several times.

Then, feeling slightly steadier, he hurried back into the apartment. The shower was hissing in the bathroom, air whining in the pipes. He dabbed cold water on his face with a paper towel and rinsed out his mouth at the kitchen sink.

Marlou was wearing only a blue towel when she came out. He stood in the bedroom doorway and watched her wrestle her damp body into panties and bra, then Levi's and a T-shirt. She had to sit on the floor to work into the Levi's. Neither of them was embarrassed. They didn't want to be by themselves. She didn't once glance at the bed, but he was sure she knew the dead animal was gone or she wouldn't have stayed in the room.

He helped her scoop clothes out of her dresser drawers and stuff them into an old red suitcase. She had enough presence of mind to choose what she wanted from the closet, handing him about a dozen dresses, slacks, and blouses, all on wire hangers.

She ran into the bathroom with a white plastic grocery bag lettered NATIONAL SUPERMARKETS in bright red, and he heard her dumping cosmetics into it.

Marlou carried the cosmetics bag, and he carried the suitcase in his right hand, the hangered clothes slung over his left shoulder. After she locked the door behind them, they tromped down the stairs and outside into the heat and sunlight. They didn't speak.

Nudger gassed up the car at a Texaco station that featured a convenience store. When he paid for the gas he bought a fresh role of antacid tablets and thumbed two of them into his mouth. Chewed them too fast and swallowed jagged fragments. He plopped more money on the counter for the acne-cursed teenage clerk, and pulled a can of Mountain Dew out of the cooler near the door. He pried up the can's pull-tab and washed down the antacid tablet fragments with the fizzy soda so his throat felt better and he could talk without it closing. Still, his eyes were watering.

When he got back in the car, Marlou had her head bowed and was silently crying. He drove around for a while, slumped behind the steering wheel and taking a pull now and then on the Mountain Dew can.

Marlou finally stopped crying and was quiet, staring straight ahead, but at something inside her skull.

Hell of a life, Nudger thought. Just a hell of a life. He squeezed the empty can so it wouldn't roll, then dropped it on the car's floor. Cut the wrong direction down some one-way streets to make sure nobody was following them.

Then he aimed the Granada's rusting hood north toward Hannibal.

18

Mark Twain this, Mark Twain that. The great writer had been dead almost a century but he was still his hometown's principal industry. Nudger wondered what Twain would say about it all if he could somehow see it. Surely it would give the old cynic a few good yuks.

Highway 36 ran through the heart of town and became 3rd Street. Nudger turned the Granada east onto Center and drove toward the river.

The riverfront was dominated by what looked like some tall, connected grain-storage tanks, lined up in a neat row like stubby missile silos ready for a launch. Beyond them was a docked excursion riverboat: dinner, music, and dancing while paddle wheels churned the Big Muddy. As might be expected near the river, that end of town seemed to be comprised mostly of industrial property, some of which had been converted to shops and small hotels. This was a tourist area, all right: antique "shoppes," cutsey restaurants, even a former brothel that had been fashioned into a hotel. Huck's river.

Nudger drove west again, then slowed the car. It didn't rattle so much at a reduced speed. He was afraid Hannibal's roughly paved streets might have messed up the suspension, but maybe the jolting ride had only loosened a few bolts here and there. What you'd expect with an old car.

He touched the brake pedal again. "That place looks good."

Marlou said, "Good as any." Her voice was flat. Vanita's funeral still weighing on her.

Nudger pulled the Granada into the lot of the Aunt Polly Motel, a U-shaped, two-story structure with an oval swimming pool in the center. The sign near the entrance was in the form of two youths standing perilously on a log raft. Nudger wondered what it looked like at night, lighted. The pool had one of those curved plastic slides with a trickle of water constantly running down it to keep the surface wet and slippery. A strikingly well-built woman in a red bathing suit was leaning with one hand on the chain-link fence surrounding the pool, watching a couple of preteen boys splashing around in the deep end beneath the diving board. She looked worried, as if she wished they'd do something less dangerous, maybe use the slide the way they had when they were seven.

"Can I swim here?" Marlou asked as they climbed out of the car. Surprised Nudger.

"Sure," he said, "so long as there are other people in the pool. But don't strike up or encourage any conversations. You oughta be safe here if you keep to yourself as much as possible."

She squinted her green eyes up at him. "We gonna register me under some other name?"

"Yeah. Romantic, isn't it? Got any ideas?"

She shook her head. "Whatever the name is, I won't have to answer to it, so it don't make any difference."

The motel office was small and paneled in knotty pine. There was a flying fish mounted on a plaque on the wall behind the registration desk. Near matching gray vinyl chairs was a table with a Mr. Coffee just like Nudger's on it. That one must work, though. Its glass pot was half full of coffee and filled the room with a fresh-dripped smell that reminded Nudger he hadn't had lunch and was hungry.

The desk clerk was an elderly woman with a pleasant moon face and thinning gray hair. Bright blue eyes behind round spectacles too small for her wide features. She looked like one of those dolls with kindly, fleshlike faces made out of soft, dried apples. Might have been Aunt Polly herself.

Nudger exchanged pleasantries with the woman, who volunteered the location of nearby restaurants and shops. He pretended Marlou was his sister, paid cash for a room, and registered her as Rebecca Thatcher. Had to have his fun.

The room was near the pool. It had orange carpet and a king-size bed, a newish color TV. Marlou gazed around, then ambled into the bathroom, which was gleaming blue-and-white tile from floor to ceiling. Clashed like hell with the carpet that stopped at its door. "Lookit there," she said, pointing to the complimentary shampoo and plastic shower cap, next to a hair dryer mounted on the wall. Aunt Polly already mothering her. "Something, huh?" She turned and smiled at Nudger, who was standing behind her. "I think I'll be okay here."

"Me too," Nudger said, "or I wouldn't try to hide you here."

They brought her clothes in from the car, and he sat on the edge of the bed and waited while she placed a few things in drawers and hung up what was on hangers. Then she stood with her hands on her hips and turned in a slow circle. He could see she was trying to settle in and feel at home. When the circle brought her around to face Nudger she said, "What was that noise?"

"My stomach. It wants lunch. Do you?"

"I could eat. Yeah." She seemed to brighten to the idea. Time healing. Vanita, this morning, already blurring in memory and dropping into the past. The human mind was a wonderful and terrible thing.

Nudger drove her to the Mark Twain Diner, a restaurant he'd noticed in town. It was in a tan brick building, had a long counter, about a dozen tables, and vinyl booths along the wide windows that looked out on the street. Just the sort of place Tom Sawyer might have hung out in, and talked Huck into spray-painting with graffiti, if he'd lived in Hannibal today.

Nudger and Marlou sat in a booth by a window. They had hamburgers and Pepsi-Colas. When they were finished eating, he sat back, slurped the remainder of his soda with the straw, then set the straw aside and began casually chomping on the cracked ice. Making quite a racket.

"Shouldn't do that," Marlou said, wiping her fingers on her napkin. "You could, like, bust a tooth that way."

"Teeth are stronger than ice," Nudger said.

"Not as a person gets older."

He wasn't sure what she meant by that. Didn't ask. Chewed on some more ice, though. It was one of his few relatively harmless habits and he didn't intend breaking it. He drew from his pocket a roll of bills held tight by a looped rubber band. Five hundred dollars. He handed it across the table to Marlou. "Expense money," he said.

She stared at the money, then stared at him with her mouth open. "Mr. Nudger—"

"It's just Nudger, remember. And that's part of the money your sister paid me. Take it. Use it as you need it."

"But you already paid for the motel room. Even one with a great big bed."

An old gray farmer-type wearing a cap that was lettered CATERPILLAR above the bill looked over at them and frowned. A dollop of ketchup dropped back onto his plate from the french fry he was holding between gnarled thumb and forefinger.

"It's okay," Nudger assured her. "Bringing you here was my idea." Was the old guy leaning toward them now, trying to eavesdrop?

Nudger lowered his voice as Marlou accepted the money and dropped it in her purse. "I'll call you tonight and leave a number where you can get hold of me."

"I got your office and home numbers."

"I won't be either of those places."

"Huh? You going, like, into hiding too?"

"I like to think of it as changing my base of operations." He couldn't tell her where he'd be, because he wasn't sure himself. "Finished eating?" he asked.

She said she, like, was.

He paid the check and slid out of the booth.

The old guy in the Caterpillar cap stared disapprovingly at Marlou as they went out, then glanced at Nudger. There was something like envy in his faded eyes.

When Nudger got back to St. Louis he told Danny he was going to be away for a while.

"Some sorta vacation, Nudge?" Danny asked, wiping down the stainless steel counter with his gray towel.

"I don't get enough business as it is," Nudger said. "Vacations are what I try to avoid. Will you keep track of who goes up to my office door and when?"

"You know I will. What friends are for. Want some coffee?"

Nudger said, "Sure, thanks." He watched as Danny worked the spigot on the complex steel urn behind the counter. The urn hissed, gurgled, and reluctantly gave up a trickle of coffee. From near the bottom, Nudger figured. Oh-oh.

He carried the cup upstairs to his office and into the half-bath, then poured it into the washbasin slowly, so Danny wouldn't hear the drain working and suspect. What friends were for.

The usual sales pitches and crank calls were on the answering machine. Also some verbal acid from Eileen, but Nudger only listened to a few words before punching the Erase button.

He hated guns, but he wished he owned one now. The Roger Bobinet effect. Nudger opened his locked bottom file drawer and peeked in the back at the belt holster lying useless on top of some file folders. He could buy a realistic toy gun, maybe fool Bobinet with that if it became necessary. The genuine spring-loaded holster would lend credibility. He might even get a water pistol, load it and squirt Bobinet and the skeleton. Then they'd all have a laugh and let bygones be bygones.

Nope, probably not.

Nudger decided to forget the toy gun idea. He shoved the drawer closed on its growling metal rollers.

All that remained now was for him to pick up some clothes at his apartment. Then he could find some out-of-the-way place to stay, where he wouldn't have to worry about following Vanita and other of nature's creatures into death at the hands of the skeleton and Roger Bobinet.

He was closing the office door, about to lock it, when the phone rang. Only the thought that he hadn't yet given Marlou another number made him answer it.

Nudger recognized the nasal, wheezing voice immediately. Not Marlou. The skeleton.

"Nudger?"

"You must be psychic," Nudger said. "I was just standing here thinking about you."

"I bet. Tried to get you earlier."

"Shoulda left a message."

"I don't ever do that. Don't like my voice on tape. Where you been, Nudger?"

"Looking for diamonds."

"Any luck?"

"Not yet, but let's set up a meeting. We can talk things over."

The skeleton laughed. "No meetings, asshole. We'll just chat by phone, or maybe turn up unexpectedly when it's time to talk face-to-face. Keep you on your toes that way."

Nudger considered punching Record on the answering machine, but he thought the machine might make some sort of microchip high-tech sound that would tip off the skeleton. Make him mad. Nudger didn't want that.

"Anything we oughta know?" the skeleton asked. "Other than you ain't located the diamonds."

"Nothing," Nudger said.

"You trying hard, Nudger? Giving it the old hundred and ten percent?"

"Of course."

"Maybe you need more incentive."

"Is there more? You threatened my life."

"Yeah, you got a point." Wheeze. Cough! "I'll call again

soon, Nudger. At your office, your apartment, or maybe at your lady friend's place."

"You won't find me at Marlou's. Probably won't find her, either. She phoned and told me she'd discovered a dead animal on her bed. And a funeral wreath. I don't know why, but she took it as some kind of warning."

The skeleton wheezed and chuckled. "Didn't mean the Marlou cunt, Nudger. Meant your *lady friend*. Assuming she's a lady." He hung up.

Nudger sat squeezing the phone so hard his hand ached. *Claudia! The skeleton had meant Claudia!*

He sat for a moment in apprehension and silence. Then he replaced the receiver. The office suddenly seemed unbearably hot and stifling, a few feet smaller all the way around.

Nudger pushed himself up out of the swivel chair, left the office, and trudged downstairs into more intense heat.

He told Danny on second thought he wasn't going anywhere after all.

19

Nudger left Danny's Donuts and went back upstairs to his office. He stayed there only long enough to phone Claudia. He wanted to make sure that if she was home, she'd remain there until he arrived.

"Nudger," she said, "you sound upset."

"Just do me the favor of staying inside and locking your door. Don't answer the phone or go to the door for anyone till I get there. Okay?"

"I was planning on driving out to Kirkwood to have dinner with a couple of other teachers from the school. We were going to play Scrabble."

"Call and cancel," Nudger said. "Please."

There was a pause at the other end of the line before she spoke. "This is all a bit melodramatic, isn't it?"

"Sure. Life gets like that sometimes. Not like Scrabble." *An English teacher; she'd be hell on wheels at Scrabble.*

She sighed.

"I wouldn't ask if I didn't think you might really be in danger."

"I know you wouldn't. I'll be here. I'll do what you suggest."
Suggest! Another sigh. "You and your fucking oddball occupation."

"All I know," Nudger said helplessly. "All I can do. You don't like it. Neither do I. Neither does my stomach."

She said, "You like it."

"In a love-hate sort of way, though. I'll stop on the way over and get carry-out for supper. Chicken McNuggets, huh?"

She laughed, then hung up before he could find out what kind of sauce she wanted. Probably she was still miffed because he'd deprived her of the opportunity to kick ass at Scrabble. There was a side to Claudia that could be fiercely competitive.

He depressed the phone's cradle button, then let it flip back up so there was a dial tone and used a pencil to peck out Hammersmith's number at the Third. Identified himself.

Hammersmith put him on hold and kept him there over a minute. Nudger sat wondering where the diamonds could be. He had to figure this out. The jewels might not have even found their way to St. Louis. Maybe he should talk to somebody in New York. He might even have to go there. He'd been there once before, about ten years ago. Towering buildings, schools of yellow taxis swimming the narrow streets, everybody on the make for everything. He hadn't seen one celebrity and didn't much like New York.

Finally there was a loud *click!* on the line.

Hammersmith said, "You sound worried, Nudge."

Claudia had picked up on his mood right away, too. Christ, was it *that* obvious? "I'm worried about Claudia. I just got a call from the skeleton. You were right, he wouldn't even talk about a meeting. And he only stayed on the phone a short time. He made sure I understood he knows about Claudia."

"Knows about her?"

"That she's my 'lady friend' as he put it. I thought at first he was talking about Marlou Dee, but he set me straight. If I don't find those diamonds, Bobinet'll go after Claudia the way he did Vanita Lane."

Hammersmith did nothing but breathe into the phone for a while. Then he said, "Shit! You tell her about it?"

"Not yet. She's locked in her apartment and I'm about to leave my office and drive over there. Can you give her some protection?"

"Sure." Hammersmith did some more hard breathing. Thinking? "Obvious protection means Bobinet and the thin guy would know you brought in the law."

"So it'll have to be plainclothes work. And some of your best. She's gotta be protected, Jack." Nudger was surprised by the desperate edge in his voice.

"Ease up, Nudge. She will be. I'll put Ervine and Hall on it."

Nudger was somewhat reassured. He didn't know who Hall was, but he knew Larry Ervine. A veteran cop who lived his job. Who treated it as more than a job. His nickname had been "Iron Guts" when he rode a patrol car. Ervine liked to pretend he was called that because of the hot Mexican food he was addicted to, not mentioning his citations for bravery. "Will Springer okay a surveillance?"

"Oh, he would if he knew about it. Claudia might draw Bobinet and the skeleton, so Springer'd see her as bait. Use her any way he could. You know Springer."

Nudger knew. He also knew that Claudia was, in effect, going to be regarded as bait anyway. The difference was that with Hammersmith running the surveillance, the emphasis would be on protecting her even if it meant losing Bobinet and the skeleton. Springer would trade Claudia for either of those two and the resulting boost to his career. Not even glance back. Springer used people and then stepped over them.

Hammersmith said, "You gonna stay with her, Nudge?"

"I'll spend this evening at her place. Tonight, too. Listen, Jack, can you get me the name of the NYPD investigating officer on the Rupert Winslow murder?"

"Hot after those diamonds, eh, Nudge?"

"Finding them's the only way I see myself getting clear of this mess."

"And you think they might still be in New York?"

"Well, it's possible. They weren't on the plane."

"Other, safer ways to transport stolen diamonds. Maybe Winslow used one of them. Such as somebody in a car. Or the U.S. mail. He was planning on flying back to St. Louis, so it doesn't make sense he'd stash the diamonds in New York."

"No, but Winslow was unpredictable, and not rocket scientist smart. Can you set me up to talk with the New York investigating officer?"

"Sure." The slurping, wheezing sound of a cigar being lighted. Nudger wondered if the noxious green smoke could somehow make it through the phone line. "Claudia going to work tomorrow?"

"I haven't talked to her about it. Knowing how she is, she'll probably give it a try."

"Let her, Nudge. We can protect her just as well out at Stowe School. Maybe better. And it wouldn't be a good idea for her to break her routine right now. That'd tip Bobinet and the skeleton. So send her off to work in the morning; we'll stay with her. Tell her not to worry; she won't see us, but we'll be there."

Nudger said, "She'll think that's melodramatic."

"Goddamn, Nudge, it is."

Less than an hour later Nudger stood holding two white McDonald's carry-out bags, waiting for Claudia to come to her door. He'd gotten a twenty-piece order of Chicken McNuggets, french fries, two large diet sodas. Every kind of sauce. The odor wafting up from the bags was making him hungry.

He heard light footsteps on the other side of the door. Claudia's voice. "That the meter reader?"

Damn her, why'd she have to joke at a time like this? For a moment he wished she'd seen Vanita Lane in the motel room. The dead canary. The mutilated animal on Marlou's bed. For only a moment. He said, "It's Nudger." Thinking the McNuggets didn't smell so good now.

She was wearing her blue terry cloth robe when she opened

the door, though it was only a little past seven o'clock. Glanced down at the McDonald's bags with their golden arches and smiled. "You weren't kidding."

"Not about anything," Nudger said, kissing her forehead as he stepped inside. It was cool in the apartment. Felt great. "Anybody knocked on the door or called?"

"Only you, white knight. I'm sure this concerns the business with the diamonds, but what specifically am I supposed to be afraid of?"

Nudger told her while he stood over the kitchen table and laid out the drinks and Styrofoam containers from the bags. Spread out napkins and myriad little plastic tear-tab containers of sauce. Barbecue. Mustard. Sweet and sour.

Claudia sat down. Ate only a few McNuggets, without bothering to dip them in sauce. She was taking this more seriously now, after hearing about Roger Bobinet and his gory warning to Marlou.

"This man is sick," she said. "A monster."

"In lamb's clothing."

Nudger finished the last of the McNuggets, then got up and went to the refrigerator. Pulled the tab on a can of Busch beer and sat back down. He belched softly, tasting the mustard sauce again.

Claudia looked at his empty soda cup, french fries wrapper, and Styrofoam McNuggets container. Then the beer. She said, "Your stomach's not going to like that."

"It's already as upset as it gets," Nudger told her. He took a pull on the can. "Fear does that to it."

Claudia said, "I'm going to work tomorrow."

"Good."

She looked a little surprised. She'd expected him to urge her to stay home.

"Hammersmith has people watching out for you," he told her. "They can do that at Stowe High School as easily as here. And if somebody else is watching you, your going to work will look normal, as if I haven't warned you and put you on guard."

She toyed with her half-full cup of soda, rotating it in the puddle of condensation it had left on the smooth table. "The police wouldn't mind if this Bobinet monster tried to kill me, would they?"

"Hammersmith'd mind."

"It'd bring Bobinet and his friend out of hiding, give the police a chance to arrest them."

"No denying that," Nudger said. "But the object's to see that you're safe. Hammersmith's sticking his neck out, doing this on his own so the priorities stay in the right order."

She smiled. So beautiful, even though her dark eyes were somber with apprehension. "Good old Jack."

"His people'll be guarding you all the time. You won't see them, but they'll be there."

She didn't say anything about melodrama.

They cleaned up the supper clutter, then Nudger phoned Marlou in Hannibal. Charged the call to his office.

Marlou answered on the third ring. He told her he was just checking to make sure she was all right.

She was fine, she assured him. Hannibal was a quiet place, but she wasn't bored. Apparently it didn't take much to keep her happy; magazines and television. Not like her sister, who'd walked the wild path.

After he'd hung up, Nudger and Claudia settled down in the living room and watched the Cardinals ball game with the Giants on TV. The game had a late starting time because it was being played on the West Coast. It soon developed into a pitchers' duel. The announcers kept referring to it as a gem.

In the bottom of the ninth, with the score tied, Will Clark hit a three-run homer and Nudger and Claudia went to bed and made love. Claudia was hesitant at first, the fear getting in the way. Then her tentativeness suddenly left her and she clung to Nudger with a fierceness he remembered from their first nights together, after he'd saved her from suicide. He climaxed a while after she did. Bowed his head to a fleeting sadness. *You're getting old, Nudger.*

He rolled onto his back, gasping, feeling his own mortality

and praying Claudia wouldn't think again of taking her life. The strain of what was happening might do that to her.

But that was silly, he decided. Claudia's psychiatrist, Dr. Oliver, had told Nudger that Claudia now had a powerful "life force," and unless clinical depression set in she was unlikely to see suicide as an alternative to solving her problems or waiting them out. Clinical depressions. Roger Bobinet had probably inspired a few of those.

She went into the bathroom, still nude. Padded back a few minutes later in her bare feet and lay down again beside him. The bedsprings sang. She wriggled close so her arm was against him, one of her toes barely making contact with his leg.

She said, "I'm glad I'm not alone, Nudger."

"So am I."

He drifted into uneasy sleep.

In the morning he kissed her good-bye and watched from the living room window as she crossed the street at an angle and walked toward where her car was parked down the block. Always he marveled at her rhythmic, elegant walk. She passed out of sight beneath the branches of a nearby maple tree.

He turned away from the window. Poured himself another cup of coffee, then went into the living room and turned on the 'Today' show on TV.

Jumped up from where he was seated on the sofa when he heard the grind of a key in the front door. The snick of the lock. Bobinet and the skeleton? Somehow? A chill spiraled up the back of his neck.

The door opened.

Claudia walked in. Stood still. Her face was pale. Without expression.

In a dreamy voice she said, "Nudger, there's a dead man sitting in my car."

20

Nudger walked outside with Claudia. Death again. The thought of it, along with the heat, hit him hard and made him nauseated, affected his stomach as if the earth were gently and relentlessly rocking. He thumbed an antacid tablet into his mouth and chewed. It helped some. Calmed the carnival ride.

They walked at a normal pace along the sun-washed side-walk, down the block toward where Claudia's toylike white Chevette was parked at the curb. A station wagon with a loud muffler rumbled past, someone on his way to work. Some of Claudia's South St. Louis neighbors were out. Older people mostly. Two women were diligently sweeping their concrete porches, another the street near the curb. Something you saw frequently in this part of town. A man in a baseball cap and sleeveless undershirt was patiently watering his zoysia grass before the sun got too hot. Everything seemed so normal that Nudger heard himself say, "You sure about this, Claudia?"

She didn't bother answering.

As they approached the car Nudger saw him. Realized why no one had noticed the man was a corpse. He was sitting up straight in the passenger's seat, wearing what looked like a porkpie hat. Now he was as out of fashion as his headgear. His head was bowed slightly, as if he were reading something in his lap, or possibly dozing. Death, so awesome, could also be so mundane.

Claudia said, "The cross-over safety belt's holding him up like that."

She stopped near the rear bumper. Nudger walked to the front of the little car and peered in through the windshield. The man's head was tilted so his face was barely visible, but his flesh had a pale, waxy look. Not dead, only sleeping?

Not likely.

Nudger opened the car door. Heat rolled out at him, along with something else that didn't smell good. The man's sphincter muscle had relaxed in death and he'd fouled himself. There was a great deal of dried blood; it appeared almost black on his white shirt front. In his lap.

Nudger straightened up, jerked his head to the side, and drew a deep breath through his mouth. Held it and stooped low so he could look more closely up at the man's face.

He moved away from the car before exhaling and breathing normally again. Left the door open. The odor followed him.

A couple of neighbors had tumbled onto the idea that something odd was occurring. The guy in the baseball cap and sleeveless undershirt, holding the hose, was staring across the street and watering his sidewalk.

Claudia said, "Know who he is—was?"

"Yeah. Ed Franks. A private investigator. Eileen's lawyer, Henry Mercato, hired him to watch us and gather evidence of our wild spending of money that should go to Eileen."

Nudger caught shadowy movement in the corner of his vision. He turned and saw a bearish man with wide, sloping shoulders approaching. The man wasn't wearing a suitcoat and his tie was loosened, his shirt's top button unfastened. Everything about him, his clothes, the flesh of his neck, his face, was wrinkled. It had been several years since they'd last seen each other, so it took Nudger a few seconds to recognize him.

Nudger said, "'Lo, Larry."

"'Lo, Nudge." Larry Ervine smiled. It made his face even more wrinkly, like folding money, but kinder and not as green. He glanced at the open car door, the unnatural turn of the passenger's leg. He knew death when he saw it, even from a distance. "What've we got here, one of those famous South St. Louis parking space disputes?"

"Dead man," Nudger said.

"His space?"

Nudger always marveled at cops' surface callousness in the presence of violent death. It was a much misunderstood protective device that helped to keep them sane in the often irrational world through which they moved.

"My friend's car," Nudger said. He cocked his head toward Ervine. "Claudia, Larry Ervine. Larry, Claudia. Larry's with the police, Claudia."

Ervine nodded politely to Claudia. "I know who you are, ma'am. Been assigned to protect you. This"—he nodded toward the corpse in the car—"musta happened last night before I came on duty."

"I just . . . found him like that," Claudia said, as if *she* might be suspected of the crime. After all, the corpse was sitting in *her* car. Nudger realized she was still in mild shock. She should be bogged in Highway 40 traffic, driving at five miles per hour to her job at Stowe High School. Instead she was still on her own street, talking with Nudger and a Homicide officer while a dead guy sat silently by her car, the door hanging open as if he'd like to overhear. Ed Franks, snooping even in death.

While Nudger chewed two more antacid tablets, Ervine strolled over to the car and squatted down to examine the body. He straightened up slowly, as if his back ached, and unhooked a small black walkie-talkie with a short, blunt aerial from his belt. Static crackled as he radioed in what he'd found. The portable unit blared something only Ervine understood.

He shot a look at the knot of people gathering on the sidewalk. He said, "Stay clear, folks," in a quiet way that caused all movement to stop. He smiled at the still, somber onlookers and walked back over to Nudger and Claudia. "Know this guy, Nudge?"

Nudger told him who Franks was, and what he might have been doing on Claudia's street.

Ervine said, "I heard of Franks. S'pose to be a real jerkoff."

"Figures," Nudger said, "considering his employer."

The high warble of approaching sirens rode the hot air like banshees in pain. Urgent. Getting closer.

The knot of neighbors stirred. Heads swiveled.

A patrol car, red and blue flashing dome lights fighting the glare of the sun, had turned the corner and was headed toward them. Another car entered the block at the opposite corner. The sirens were deafening for a few seconds, then cut to silence. They didn't growl down like the older sirens.

There were few parking spaces, so the two dusty blue cruisers braked nose to nose in the middle of the street. Car doors opened and slammed shut. Uniforms piled out and began the systematic process of lending order to the chaotic aftermath of murder. It made things at least *seem* comprehensible, though often they weren't.

The police were setting up red-and-white barriers at each end of the block. The familiar yellow crime scene ribbons were unfurled, strung in a rough rectangle that encompassed Claudia's car. Blue uniforms everywhere. Busy, busy. Inside the car, Franks seemed almost alive and totally unconcerned that he was the cause of all this fuss.

An unmarked Pontiac angled to the curb near where a couple of uniforms were holding back the curious crowd. Its doors opened simultaneously. Hammersmith eased his bulk out from the passenger's side with his incongruous grace. He went over and examined Franks as if paying his respects. Wrinkled his nose at the stench and fired up a cigar. Maybe situations like this were the reason he smoked the foul-smelling abominations. He stood well away from the car and puffed and puffed. Then, like a fat genie emerging from a mystic cloud of smoke, he glided toward Nudger.

He said, "Our friend Franks keeps turning up, eh?"

"Won't anymore," Nudger said.

Hammersmith, still wearing an expression of distaste, drew on the cigar and then blew a thunderous green cloud. He glanced back at Franks and said, "You kill him, Claudia?"

Claudia gripped Nudger's arm and her body stiffened. Then she realized Hammersmith was joking in his macabre way and Nudger felt her relax beside him. She said, "I never saw him before. Didn't know who he was till Nudger told me."

"He was killed by Bobinet to warn us to stay in line," Nudger said.

Hammersmith said, "Franks had no real connection to the diamond thing."

"Bobinet and the skeleton wouldn't know that for sure. Here's this guy sneaking around keeping an eye on me and Claudia, so it figured to them he had an angle. They know from nothing about the sharklike behavior of Henry Mercato and Eileen. They probably questioned Franks, saw his ID, and maybe even bought his story. But they couldn't let him live, so they decided to make him an object lesson and a warning. Like the dog."

Hammersmith sucked on his cigar. "Whashat? Dog?"

Nudger told him about the disemboweled dog on Marlou Dee's bed.

Hammersmith said, "Hmm." Withdrew his cigar from his mouth and stared down at it. As if talking to it, he said, "Looks like to me that Franks was what you might call gutted. Disemboweled."

"God," Claudia said. "Killed like a dog and for the same sick reason."

"Humane Society'd object," Hammersmith said. Nudger knew he could carry his cops' humor too far, get Claudia mad. Didn't want that to happen.

"I spent the night here," he said. "When Claudia left the apartment to get in her car and go to work, she found Franks. They must have done him and set him up in the car last night, before Ervine came on stakeout."

"I expect the M.E.'s estimated time of death'll bear that

out," Hammersmith said. "Ervine wouldn't have missed this business if he'd been around at the time. Other cops, maybe, but not him. Way it looks, Franks was killed someplace else. Then the killers probably drove up next to Claudia's car and transferred the corpse. It'd only take them seconds, not minutes. There's a lot of blood in the street, and some down in the grass on the passenger side of the car."

"Hell of a lot of nerve," Nudger said.

"You mean because of the way people feel about their lawns around here?"

"You know what I mean. Takes balls to move around a dead body like they did."

"Naw, not really. On a dark residential street. Even if somebody happened to hear the noise and see them, they'd figure it was a couple of guys dealing with a drunk friend."

Claudia leaned on Nudger and said, "I'm feeling lightheaded. Mind if I go upstairs and sit down?"

"The both of you go," Hammersmith said. "I'll be up in a while and question you in more detail, make it official."

Nudger took Claudia's arm and began leading her down the street toward her apartment. She was trembling and didn't seem to know it.

Behind him Hammersmith said, "Better haul ass, Nudger, before Springer shows up."

Sound advice, Nudger thought.

As soon as they entered the apartment, he guided Claudia directly to the bathroom. He helped her kneel on the tile floor in front of the toilet bowl. Worshiping the porcelain god, drunks called this. Whatever it was called, might as well get it over with.

Without looking up, she said, "I think I'm gonna be okay, Nudger. Really."

Sure you are.

He was tasting metal, and his own stomach was fluttering, but he figured he could keep his breakfast where it belonged. The antacid tablets had helped. And he hadn't happened on Franks as a gruesome surprise, the way Claudia had.

Odd, he thought, that he'd puked after dealing with a dead dog, but Franks, the agent of Eileen and Mercato, didn't affect him as strongly even though he and Nudger were of the same species. Even the same profession. But then he hadn't had to fit Franks's corpse into a plastic trash bag and dispose of it.

His stomach did give a kick, and he chased colorful visions of the dog, and of Franks, from his mind.

Soaked with icy sweat, he stood at the washbasin and twisted the Cold handle. Got a damp washcloth ready while Claudia retched.

He didn't watch her directly but kept his eyes fixed on her bent and heaving back in the mirror.

21

After Hammersmith and Springer had gone, Nudger and Claudia sat on the sofa in her living room. Claudia had just hung up the phone, after explaining to someone at Stowe High School what had happened, and assuring them that she'd be there for her afternoon class. She had an hour before she was due to leave, so she was sipping a Diet Pepsi, trying to cool mind and body before venturing back out into the difficult and unpredictable world.

Nudger was pulling on Busch beer from a can. He had his legs stretched out and crossed at the ankles. His throat was sore from talking so much to Hammersmith and Springer. Springer, mainly, with his back-door, insinuating questions. Weasely little bastard.

At least Hammersmith had gotten off the pin by telling Springer that he'd planned to inform him of the protective surveillance on Claudia, only there hadn't been time. Franks had been considerate enough to be murdered on the first night, thus providing Hammersmith with a plausible enough explanation for moving behind Springer's back.

It was almost noon; the glaring sun was bent through the slanted venetian blinds above the laboring air conditioner and couldn't penetrate more than mere inches into the apartment. It was cool and dim in Claudia's living room. Sanctuary, now that Springer and Hammersmith had left.

Nudger looked over at Claudia, thought how much he loved her, and said, "Ever think about seeing Jamaica?"

She stared at him. "The two of us?"

"No, just you."

She thought about that, her lean face serious. Then she shook her head, causing her long dark hair to swing in a soft pendulum motion. "I can't run from this, Nudger."

He figured he'd hear that from her; she'd done a complete turnaround since her suicide attempt and a few years of psycho-analysis. Dr. Oliver had transformed her into a quiet fighter. Nudger decided to try reason. "Franks should have run."

"That's obvious. But Franks doesn't teach two remedial English classes to learning-impaired children."

"Your job can't be *that* important, Claudia! We're talking about your life here."

"*My* life. That's the point. I'll live it my way, without being dictated to by a couple of scumbag terrorists."

"These guys left a corpse in your car, Claudia!"

"I remember." She calmly sipped Pepsi.

Nudger said, "Jesus!"

She gazed at him over the rim of her glass; dark eyes so deep. Like wells to the earth's core and mystery. She set the glass down on the table by the sofa. "You're more or less in my position, Nudger. Are *you* running?"

"No. Because I've been hired to do a job." Oh-oh, shouldn't have said that.

She smiled like a fisherman who's set the hook. "So have I been hired to do a job. And I intend to continue doing it."

"God, you're stubborn!" he said in frustration.

"Now there's a quality you should understand."

"Christ, Claudia, be reasonable!"

"Even if you're not?"

"That's never stopped you before."

"Nudger, it's gallant of you to be so concerned. But life's not a John Wayne movie, and you're not a hell of a lot like John Wayne anyway. I'll be okay."

Hey! He felt a pang of resentment. "More like Clark Gable?"

"Well, a little more. When he was older."

He felt better, but not much.

"I'll be safe enough," she assured him. "Hammersmith's continuing the watch on me. And after what happened to Franks, I'll be extra careful. I promise."

Nudger knew he wasn't going to change her mind. "I'll drive you out to the school." The police had impounded her car. After they released it, the interior would have to be cleaned as thoroughly as possible. Even then, something of Franks might haunt it. She should get another car.

"All right," she told him. "But I can catch a ride home with a teacher who lives in Bellville." She stood up and smoothed her dress. Smiled at him, then leaned over and kissed the top of his head where his hair was thinning. "Nudger, don't worry so much about me. Please."

He didn't answer. Finished his beer in one long series of swallows and stood up. "You ready to leave?"

"Soon as I get my briefcase."

Nudger remembered the relationship of his father and mother. Dad working, Mom tending house and kids. His mother had never uttered the phrase "my briefcase."

The world had changed and was still changing, dragging Nudger along with it. Sometimes reluctantly.

As he recalled, the same thing had happened to Clark Gable.

After dropping off Claudia at Stowe School, Nudger drove to his office. He checked in with Danny, who was leaning behind the counter and studying a grease-spotted sports page from the morning paper. Nudger saw an upside-down photo of a sliding ballplayer.

Danny folded the paper and said, "Cards got a chance at the pennant if lightning strikes all the Mets."

Nudger thought that was about right, but lightning had been known to strike the weak as well as the strong.

Danny told him there hadn't been any upstairs callers. No one had entered the door next to the doughnut shop's and climbed the steps to Nudger's office door. Situation normal.

Nudger forced down a Dunker Delite for lunch and refused Danny's offer of coffee. Had a cup of water with cracked ice instead. "My stomach's pitching a fit," he explained to Danny, who believed him. Generous and naive Danny.

Chewing on the small chunks of ice, Nudger climbed the stairs to his office and switched on the air conditioner. He slapped it before it could begin making its peculiar noise. What was wrong with the damned thing? How long would it continue to work?

He opened the window directly behind the desk for a few minutes to let the hot air out.

That seemed to let even hotter air in, so he promptly closed the window and sat down. He noticed the glowing numeral 1 on his answering machine and pressed the Play button.

The message was from Hammersmith, giving him the name of the New York City police detective who'd handled the Rupert Winslow suicide—as it was still officially called.

Nudger swiveled around in his chair and stared out the window at the pigeons perched on a ledge of the building across the street. Just as well he didn't own a gun; he'd be tempted to take a shot at one of the defecating rats of the air. He sometimes wondered why he hated pigeons so much. Attacked by a flock of them as an infant? Maybe. He swiveled back around and direct-dialed the New York number Hammersmith had left on the machine.

The detective's name was Rico Stompano. Nudger thought it more suitable for a gangster than a cop. But then he'd known a cop named Al Capone, so what the heck.

Stompano didn't disappoint. He sounded like a TV actor's idea of a Brooklyn hoodlum.

After fencing with Nudger for a while he told him the Winslow case was still open, in light of facts trickling out of St.

Louis, and from the FBI, who were still tangentially involved because of the airliner bombing. "You know how long it takes this kinda thing to wind down," Stompano said, as if Nudger were always slogging through this sort of mine field. The Mike Hammer of the Midwest.

"Is there anything that suggests Winslow might have gotten the diamonds to St. Louis, or anywhere out of New York?" Nudger asked.

"Nothin' even to suggest diamonds," Stompano said. He sounded bored. Tolerating Nudger. New York, Nudger figured.

"You buying the idea of suicide?" Nudger asked. "I mean, personally buying it?"

"I ain't even considering it," Stompano said, "bein' still a young man with lots to live for. But I guess you mean in regards to Rupert Winslow. Tell you, Nudger, I don't buy this or buy that, I just do my fuckin' job. Put the facts together, see what picture they make, stop off and have a beer and then go home. You know?"

Nudger said he knew. "Lots of money involved here; how come there's no pressure on you people to solve this one?"

Stompano laughed. "You ever walk through the diamond district in Manhattan, Nudger? Fuckin' zillions of dollars worth of stones winkin' like whores' eyes in the show windows. Not to mention how many more behind the counters, in the safes. Million bucks worth of diamonds don't amount to much when you put it in perspective. I mean, it's a shit-pot fulla money, but not when you're talkin' figures make the national deficit seem small. The merchants ain't all that upset since insurance is reimbursing the loss. The insurance company now, outfit called Sloan Trust, they're pissing bullets over the loss."

"I met their representative," Nudger said. "Bill Stockton."

"Yeah, I know Stockton." Stompano's tone suggested he didn't think much of the insurance investigator.

Nudger asked Stompano to let him know if any information on the diamonds did turn up.

"Goes both ways," Stompano said. "You let me know, huh? Somethin' interesting pops up on your end?"

Nudger said sure, that went without saying.

Stompano said, "Anything else I can do ya?"

"Nope."

"Take care, pal." Stompano hung up.

Nudger sat for a while and absently chewed what was left of the cracked ice in his cup, setting up a hell of a racket inside his skull. He tried to imagine being Rupert Winslow in a hotel room with a million dollars worth of stolen diamonds. Tried to imagine what he'd do with those diamonds if he chose to double-cross his partners in crime.

But he couldn't be Rupert Winslow, even in his imagination. Couldn't let himself identify with someone who was dead. Like asking for trouble.

22

At four o'clock Nudger drove to Claudia's to make sure she'd arrived home from work. As he turned onto Wilmington he saw Larry Ervine sitting in a parked unmarked Plymouth down the block from her apartment. He nodded to Ervine as he drove past, then found a shaded parking space for the Granada almost in front of Claudia's building.

As Nudger climbed out of the car, the low but glaring sun made his eyes ache. Heat rolled out from beneath the Granada, across his feet and ankles. He wondered how Ervine could put up with sitting in the unmarked police car, only now and then running the engine and air conditioner. Sometimes Nudger was glad he was no longer a cop.

As he walked toward the apartment building, he noticed there were fewer people than usual out tending lawns or cars. Faces appeared at windows, however, eyes curious, as if this morning had been only a preview and they didn't want to miss the feature attraction. Thought it might be Nudger.

Claudia must have seen him, or maybe heard him clomping

up the stairs and glanced outside and seen the Granada. She opened the door before he had a chance to knock.

He kissed her on the lips and she kissed him back hard. Then she backed away, a little breathless, and said, "See, I'm still in one piece."

"And a beautiful one." She'd changed into a plain white blouse, Levi's like Marlou Dee wore only not so tight. Claudia could wriggle into hers standing up; he'd seen her do it.

She closed and locked the door behind him, and he watched her sway across the room and perch on the arm of the sofa. Such a walk. She was smiling at him, but it was an uneasy smile, weak around the corners.

He went into the kitchen to get a can of beer from the refrigerator, saw that there was none, and settled for a glass of tap water instead. He managed to wrest a couple of ice cubes from the refrigerator and dropped them into the glass.

Claudia was still sitting on the sofa arm when he returned to the living room, but her smile was gone.

He said, "I saw Larry Ervine parked down the block, watching the apartment."

"Good. He seems a capable man. Something about him I trust."

"He's good at his work," Nudger said. "You can be sure there's someone watching the back of the building, too."

"I imagine they're more alert after . . . what happened to Franks. So I'm well looked after, Nudger. That should put your mind at ease."

He thought about the skeleton and Roger Bobinet. "Only somewhat."

She stood up straight and slipped her hands in the pockets of her Levi's, posed in her hip-shot kind of slouch he found so graceful. "Hammersmith phoned," she said. "He told me they're finished with my car downtown and I can pick it up. Want to drive me to get it? Follow me back?"

"If your car's the way it was this morning, you might not want to drive it."

"Hammersmith had it cleaned for me. Said it'd be done around five."

"You're getting special service," Nudger said. The police had impounded his car last year. Hadn't cleaned it. Left it a mess, in fact, parked in front of an expired meter with a ticket tucked under the wiper. The law not falling evenly on all citizens.

Claudia said, "Hammersmith's a gentleman." She actually sounded serious. Nudger didn't answer.

"Should we let Detective Ervine know where we're going?" she asked.

"No. If we stop and talk to him it'd just serve to point him out to whoever else could be in the neighborhood and interested. Ervine'll see us leave, and he'll either follow or have a backup unit tailing us. Best thing you can do for him is forget he's there."

"Or he might end up like Franks . . ." she said with a quaver in her voice, as if suddenly realizing the danger involved. Death and diamonds didn't make for light-hearted games.

Nudger said, "It's an occupational risk he understands. He's also capable of dealing with it a lot better than a guy like Franks."

But the thought of Ervine dying like Franks had sobered Claudia. They went downstairs and walked silently to Nudger's car, through golden sunlight thick as water.

He drove down Wilmington in the direction away from where Ervine was sitting in the parked Plymouth, so she wouldn't look over at him as they passed.

As Nudger made a left turn on Grand Avenue, Claudia said, "Franks had a wife and son. It said so on the TV news."

Great. He switched lanes and passed a lumbering bus that had halitosis.

"The world can turn to shit in a hurry," Claudia said.

She sounded morose. He didn't like that tone in her voice at all.

After a while he said, "I've got somebody, too. I don't want to lose her."

The police garage had sent her car out somewhere to be cleaned. The little white Chevette even seemed to have been waxed. There was what looked like a white sheet over the bucket seat on the driver's side. The attendant at the garage explained that the upholstery was still damp. The inside of the car smelled like disinfectant, and there was a little scented green cutout shaped like a pine tree dangling from the rearview mirror. Hammersmith's influence.

Claudia lowered herself into the car and peered around the interior. Seemed pleased. She said to Nudger, "Meet you back at the apartment." Yanked the door shut and started the engine. He heard the compressor kick in and whine beneath the hood as she switched on the air conditioner.

When he didn't move she cranked down the window. "Something wrong, Nudger?"

"Sure you wanna drive that car? You can take the Granada."

"I can't afford to trade," she said, "so I might as well get used to driving this one even though it might be haunted."

Nudger grinned down at her. "You're something, you know that?"

"A hungry something." She wound the window back up, then immediately rolled it halfway down again. "Let's get some supper while we're out, okay?"

"Sure. I could eat."

They stopped at Maggie O'Brien's on Market Street and had the corned beef special and beer. Cheesecake and coffee for dessert. There was piped-in Irish music. Something about a free Ireland and the Irish Republican Army. Another world with other problems and players. No concern of Nudger's; he was having trouble orbiting smoothly in his own universe.

He wondered if Eileen and Mercato had hired anyone to replace Franks. It was possible. It gave Nudger perverse satisfaction knowing that, after what had happened to Franks, the price would be high. On the other hand, Mercato might be successful in dragging him back into court and he, Nudger, might eventually have to pay that price. The world sure wasn't fair. Nudger wished he were more religious and could regard life as some kind of test that if passed would guarantee celestial reward. If the tests were graded on the curve.

When they got back to Claudia's apartment he called Marlou at Aunt Polly's Motel in Hannibal. He asked how was she doing. How were things in Mark Twain country, heart of America.

She seemed a bit more restless, which was to be expected. "This is just a little old town," she said. "Not much to see or do. But there's, like, a really neat riverboat here. I sure'd love to take an excursion cruise on it. They serve food and drink and all."

Nudger wondered what they served beyond food and drink that qualified as "and all," but he didn't ask. Marlou sounded as if she might be on vacation. "Stay close to your room," he said. "Remember what we found on your bed here in St. Louis. The man who left it there killed Vanita and now he's killed somebody else."

It took her a moment to focus on what he'd said. "Gawd, no! Who'd he kill?"

"Man named Franks. A dectective who was watching me."

"But *you're* a detective." She sounded confused. Well, he couldn't blame her. "Wait a minute, wasn't that the name of the man I had the run-in with at my apartment?"

He said, "Same Franks. What he was doing when he got killed had nothing to do with the diamonds or your sister's murder, but the man who killed him didn't know that."

"You sure?"

"Positive." *As only a fool can be.* "But I hope it causes you to be careful up there."

"Oh, I been careful. Only place I go is, like, out to get something to eat, or pick up a magazine to read, or to walk around some so as to stretch my legs. Listen, Mr. Nudger, you made any progress in finding them diamonds so this can all be over?"

"Some, I think. I'm working at it, Marlou."

"I'm sure you are."

"Stay close to Aunt Polly," Nudger told her, "and when I come get you we'll take a cruise on that riverboat."

"Will do, Mr. Nudger. When you gonna call again?"

"Tomorrow. There's something I want you to write down. Got a pencil?"

She made him wait a minute, then came back on the line. "Ready an' waitin', pencil in hand."

"Here's another number where you can reach me." He gave her Claudia's phone number.

When he'd hung up, Claudia said, "Who's Aunt Polly?" Nudger told her.

She said, "So diamonds are missing and people are dying and the police are watching over me, and I suppose you're going to spend the evening and night here."

"Good supposing."

"Nudger, I'm grateful for everything being done for me. I really am."

"Especially the spending-the-night part?"

She grinned. "Yeah, especially that."

While Claudia sat at the dining room table grading English exams, he settled down on the sofa and used the remote to switch on the TV. Ran through the channels until he found the Cards-Cubs game.

So a baseball diamond was the only kind he could find. It was better than nothing.

23

Nudger didn't sleep well that night. He stood on the sidewalk the next morning with fuzz in his mouth and sand under his eyelids and watched Claudia drive down Wilmington on her way to work. Saw Ervine's relief, a cop he didn't know, follow in the same unmarked Plymouth Ervine had been sitting in last night; it had red paint scrapings on the left rear door.

The sun began beating on his head like a hot hammer, so Nudger trudged back upstairs to the apartment. Claudia had known he'd had a restless night and let him sleep this morning. Later than he'd planned, he'd thrown on his pants, undershirt, and shoes without socks, to walk her outside to her car.

Back in the apartment, he undressed again and went into the bathroom, twisted the porcelain faucet handles in the shower to full blast, then adjusted the water temperature to lukewarm. He stepped into the tub behind the stiff plastic shower curtain, a new one with a yellow daisy pattern.

Standing motionless, he let the blasting needles of water crash against his face and body. Slowly he came all the way awake as the hot water ran out and the shower gradually became cool. He applied soap to his body and rinsed off quickly, knowing the cool water might suddenly become unbearably icy. He'd been tricked before by the eccentric plumbing in Claudia's apartment.

After he toweled himself dry and got dressed, he went into the kitchen and opened the refrigerator. He stood staring at some eggs in a bowl on the middle shelf. They seemed more like unborn chickens this morning than eggs. What they were, actually, inside those shells. Yuk.

He'd learned to pay heed to the morning warnings of his delicate stomach. He settled for a tall glass of orange juice and a cup of black coffee before locking the apartment behind him and driving to his office.

When he arrived, Bill Stockton was waiting for him in the doughnut shop. A Dunker Delite with only one bite out of it lay on a white paper napkin before him. Apparently he learned fast. A survivor.

Leaving the wounded Dunker Delite behind, Stockton followed Nudger upstairs to the office.

When Nudger sat down behind the desk, Stockton remained standing. He was wearing pleated black slacks today and a snappy gray-and-white checked sport coat with silver buttons. Blue striped shirt and a blue tie with so much silk content it glittered like metal. Last time they'd met, Stockton had affected the Wall Street broker look; now he looked ready to sell junk cars instead of junk bonds. Nudger got the uneasy feeling Stockton had dressed down for this conversation, maybe to communicate with Nudger on Nudger's low level.

Nudger saw little difference between an insurance investigator and a private detective. He thought, Fuck it. He leaned back in his squealing swivel chair and laced his fingers behind his head. Waited.

Stockton's fleshy but curiously birdlike features were unreadable. He ran the back of his hand across his forehead and glanced at the air conditioner. Nudger made no move to switch the unit on.

Stockton said, "I read about Franks's death in the paper. We're not playing with Eagle Scouts, huh?"

"You surprised? After what they did to Vanita Lane?"

"No," Stockton said. "Which is kinda what brings me here. This thing is getting nastier by the day, Nudger, and I'm afraid someone else is going to die. Count those poor people on the airliner, and already the death toll's goddamned horrendous."

Nudger couldn't argue with that and didn't. He sat listening to the traffic swish past two stories below on Manchester. People on their way here and there, some of them rolling toward trouble.

"I've been in contact with my employer, Sloan Trust," Stockton said. "Way this works, they contract me to find the missing insured property—in this case, the stolen diamonds— and if my investigation leads to the recovery, my fee's ten percent of the insured amount. In this case, since the diamonds are insured for slightly more than a million, my commission'd be a little over a hundred thousand dollars. Nothing to sneeze at."

Nudger said, "I didn't sneeze. Nose didn't even itch."

"They pay me that much because I'm good at my work." There was unmistakable pride in Stockton's voice. "And to be good at the kinda work I do, sometimes you have to step outside what unenlightened people might think of as regular channels."

Ah! Nudger thought. He already had an idea what Stockton had in mind.

"Even half my commission'd mean a lot to my bank account. I'm sure it'd mean even more to yours." Stockton paused for a moment and let the drift of his words reach Nudger. He ran his fingertips down the lapel of the checkered sport coat. It wasn't his style at all; he looked like a banker dressed like a barker. "Point is, Nudger, I have permission from my company to cut you in on the commission if you were to lead me to the diamonds and save them a million dollars." He smiled unctuously. "Makes sense all around, huh?"

"Would if I knew the location of the diamonds."

Stockton's smile stayed pasted on. "I think you do know where they are."

"Yeah, I guess you must, or you wouldn't be here."

"This is a good deal for you, Nudger. Maybe the deal of your lifetime. You won't be able to get more'n twenty cents on the dollar for those diamonds from a fence. And then you gotta worry the rest of your life about the law coming down on your ass. Gotta tell you, that's no way to live."

"Why do you think I know where the diamonds are?"

"Because I've turned over every rock in the New York area, and believe me, I know where they are and what lives under them."

"And what lives under them wasn't wearing diamonds?"

"Exactly. I'd bet . . . well, I *am* betting fifty thousand dollars those diamonds aren't in New York. I say they're in St. Louis. I say you know where."

"How would I have found out?"

"From Vanita Lane, before she died. After all, the last man known to possess the stones, Rupert Winslow, was her lover."

"Hadn't been for a while, though."

Stockton shook his head almost sadly. "I told you, it's not smart to believe what Vanita says—said. Trust me, the woman was a pathological liar."

"So was Rupert Winslow. That's why they called him Ropes. Maybe he lied to her."

Stockton shoved his hands in his pockets and seemed to think about that. Rupert Winslow had conned his way into Vanita's affections, and she'd been able to lie with the best. Then Stockton snorted through his beaklike little nose. "No, Nudger. So maybe Winslow lied to her; that still doesn't put the diamonds in New York."

"Not necessarily in St. Louis, either."

"Now there's where we disagree. I know how people like Winslow think. They're like beasts of prey who roam within the confines of familiar hunting territory. He was St. Louis connected. Believe me, if the diamonds aren't in New York, they found their way to St. Louis."

" 'If,' you said."

"Oh, nothing in this world's for sure. I admit I'm theorizing. But that's how I make my living, by theorizing my way to where I need to be. Which in this case is sitting on top of the truth."

Nudger said, "I'd be happy to split your commission with you, but really I don't know where the diamonds are."

"Would your feelings be hurt if I said I didn't believe you?"

"Not like I've been turned down for the prom, no. I don't care whether you believe me."

Stockton cocked his head sharply to the side and puffed out his barrel chest. Looked more than ever like he belonged in an aviary. "Okay, Mr. Nudger. But my offer stands. If something jolts your memory and you want your fianancial problems solved, give me a call, huh? You've got my card." He buttoned the gaudy sport coat and moved confidently toward the door. He figured he had his beak in Nudger now; money talked, and it would keep talking fifty thousand dollars' worth even after he'd left the office. Money was persistent.

He stopped suddenly and turned. "By the way, you got any idea where Marcy Lou Dee is?"

"Not much of one. Why?"

"I've been trying to get in touch with her. Wanna speak to her about her sister. And about the diamonds."

"You'll be wasting your time. She's one of life's unfortunate innocents."

"Norman Rockwell's dead, Nudger. There's no such thing as innocence where money's concerned. Just people haven't had the opportunity. That's one of the prices we pay for living in the land of upward mobility. So I still wanna talk with her."

"If I see her," Nudger said, "I'll let her know."

"Obliged," Stockton said. He proudly puffed up his chest again and strutted out the door.

As if he'd found a worm.

24

Nudger spent the morning in his office, paying the bills in his Way Past Due pile, shuffling other bills from the Due to the Past Due pile. He couldn't help but muse that with fifty thousand dollars he could wipe out all his pesky creditors with a few swipes of the pen. Mightier than the sword for sure.

If he knew how to find the diamonds.

After a gastronomically daring bowl of chili at the B&L Diner down the street from the office, he sat and chewed antacid tablets and thought about where the diamonds might be. People didn't hide a million dollars' worth of gems just anywhere, so a certain psychology should apply. Let's get into someone's mind here. Suppose Vanita stashed the diamonds in Marlou's apartment without telling Marlou? It was possible. Vanita had been more than devious enough to do such a thing.

Nudger paid for the chili, dismounted his counter stool, and walked back out into the summer glare and heat. The exhaust fumes of passing cars rose wavering like taunting spirits. Someday this city was going to get hot enough for spontaneous combustion.

He strode back to where the Granada was parked across the street from his office. Waved to Danny and hand-signaled that he was leaving. Danny waved back through the grease-spotted doughnut shop window, and Nudger climbed into the Granada and drove to Marlou's apartment.

He remembered a chain lock on the inside of her door, but the only lock that would be set would be the cheap apartment latch built into the doorknob. Did burglars manufacture those things?

Nudger was prepared to use his expertise and his honed Visa card to slip the lock, but when he inserted the plastic card between door and frame he met little resistance. Knew at once the door was unlocked.

Oh-oh.

He rotated the knob and pushed the door open, his heart hammering and his stomach looping and diving. Surely there was something else he could be doing for a living. He'd better start paying more attention to the insides of matchbooks.

The air in the apartment was hot and stale. Gave the impression no one had been there for a while. But there was no way to be sure.

Nudger stepped all the way inside and saw that the living room was a mess. Pictures had been removed from the wall and smashed. The chair and sofa were overturned and their upholstery slashed. A cheap floor lamp was bent and broken. Even the curtains had been ripped partly from the windows and were hanging like shrouded figures next to the slanted venetian blinds.

"Go eeeeeasy!" Nudger's stomach warned. If there was anyone else in the apartment they might have heard it.

Nudger walked quietly on the balls of his feet to the short hall leading to the other rooms. He glanced in the bathroom. A mess there, too. Towels heaped on the floor, plastic shower curtain torn and dangling, the acrid scent of spilled soap or shampoo.

He reached Marlou's closed bedroom door and stood listening.

The silence seemed to buzz and after a while became more ominous.

Swallowing hard, he rotated the knob and swung the door open.

The bedroom was empty. It was also disarranged like the living room, only more violently. Drawers had been pulled from the dresser and turned upside down, then flung to the side against a wall. So hard that one of them had split apart. The contents of the drawers were scattered and trampled. Clothes from the closet were heaped on the floor. The bedding had been stripped from the mattress, and the mattress itself was slashed so that its stuffing bulged like the internal organs of the dog that had so recently lain dead on it. Recollection of the dog made Nudger realize the stench of its death still clung to the room. Made his stomach lurch.

He started to back toward the door, and something brushed his ear, startling him.

He whirled and saw that the Raggedy Ann doll that had been propped against Marlou's pillow was hanging from the ceiling fixture in the center of the room. A length of coarse brown twine had been twisted around its neck and yanked tight. The other end of the twine was looped around the bare light bulb. The doll's head was cocked at a sharp angle, and with its wide button eyes it actually did look as if it had been strangled.

Nudger left the bedroom and stood in the center of the ruined living room. There was something about the hanged doll that struck a chord in him and made him shudder. Roger Bobinet apparently had a macabre sense of humor. Should be no surprise.

In the sunlight angling in through the blinds, Nudger considered what he was looking at. For a moment he thought of Bill Stockton and ambition and greed. But even if Stockton was thinking along the same lines as Nudger and had searched Marlou's apartment, he wouldn't have searched so violently. And he didn't seem the type to lynch Raggedy Ann. Bobinet and the skeleton had been here, no doubt. And from the thoroughness of the destruction it appeared they hadn't found what they were looking for. Which meant it would be pointless for Nudger to comb the wreckage.

Thinking about how Marlou would feel when it came time to return to her apartment, he absently righted the upended chair. There. Better. He took a last look around. He could see the shadow of the hanged doll through the open bedroom door.

Suppressing the wave of dread and anger that ran through him, he left the apartment. He didn't see much use in locking the door now, but locked it anyway.

When he'd parked the Granada and was jogging across Manchester toward his office, he glanced into the doughnut shop and saw it was empty. Nothing unusual about that. The ratio of doughnuts to customers at Danny's was astronomical. But even Danny himself wasn't visible behind the counter, and the CLOSED sign wasn't hanging on the door.

Nudger bounced up onto the curb and strode across the sidewalk. Pushed through the door into the doughnut shop. Heat and sugary aroma hit him.

He glanced around. "Danny?"

There was a garbled reply from somewhere.

Nudger walked around the counter on his way to the back of the shop.

And almost tripped over Danny.

He was lying on his back behind the counter. His hands and feet were tied with strips of the grayish towel he usually had tucked in his belt. His face was swollen and purple and his eyes were rolling desperately. Again he made the garbled, gagging sound.

Nudger said, "Goddammit!" and knelt down beside him. Rage and pity turned to near-panic when he saw the nasty welt on Danny's throat.

Only it wasn't just a welt. Peering closer, Nudger saw that the same kind of coarse twine used to hang Raggedy Ann had been looped around Danny's neck, pulled tight, and knotted. It was imbedded deep in his flesh.

Nudger said, "Hold on, Danny!" and tried to loosen the knot. No way to do that. He attempted inserting a finger beneath where the twine was knotted. Felt the twine dig into his fingertip. Danny's eyes bugged out and he began banging the floor with his feet. Christ, the twine was tight, almost hidden in tortured flesh.

Helpless, enraged, Nudger straightened up and looked around. Moved toward the phone to dial 911, then saw a knife behind the counter. Grabbed it and held the sharp edge flat against Danny's neck and the twine. "Jesus, I'm sorry, Danny!"

Danny blinked and gazed up at him like a man staring from underwater.

Nudger began a gentle sawing motion with the knife. Blood ran. Nudger's stomach flipped. Danny moaned and his sad basset-hound eyes widened in pain. Nudger couldn't help it; he closed his eyes as he continued the sawing motion. *Don't press too hard! Movement, not depth.*

He felt resistance now. Peeked to see progress. But blood had obscured the twine. Oh, Christ!

Blood was all over Nudger's right hand. Staring at it, he became light-headed and almost fainted. Danny's face was even more purple. His teeth were clenched and his lips were drawn tight in a rictus of agony.

Sorry, Danny!

Keep the blade moving.

The twine snapped apart, flicking blood up on Nudger's face. He didn't care.

There was a noise like a jet taking off. Danny sucking in air. Another harsh intake of breath. Another. A hoarse voice said, "Nudge . . ."

"Take it easy, Danny. Stay down." Danny had begun trying to sit up despite his bound wrists and ankles. Blood was streaming down his neck and chest, but not so thickly that it seemed any major artery had been severed.

Nudger used the knife again to cut the strips of towel. Danny curled on his side in the fetal position, rubbing the welts left on his wrists by the strips of cloth.

"Stay down," Nudger said again. "I'm just going over to the phone, and I'll be back. Can you understand me?"

Danny gave a kind of nod. It seemed to hurt his neck. Nudger decided not to ask for any more answers. He shuffled sideways to the far end of the counter and picked up the phone. Dialed 911 and explained to the emergency operator that someone was injured. He gave her the address and the doughnut shop phone number.

She called back less than a minute after he'd hung up, checking the authenticity of his call, interrupting him as he was kneeling and holding a compress of paper napkins against where he'd cut Danny's neck. He was about to get profane with the operator when she hung up again.

She'd taken him him seriously, though. In less than five minutes Nudger heard sirens. A red-and-white emergency ambulance coasted to a halt in front of the doughnut shop. Doors slammed.

The two paramedics who came bursting in were efficient. They had Danny bandaged and on a gurney in no time. Danny's face was more red than purple now. Surely a better sign.

As they were wheeling him out and trying to fit an oxygen mask over his face, he was croaking, "Tell 'em at the hospital I got medical insurance. Not to worry, I got insurance."

Nudger wasn't sure if that was true. He hung the CLOSED sign on the doughnut shop door, then got in the Granada and followed the yowling ambulance to St. Mary's Hospital to help perpetuate the bluff.

25

The hospital bundled Danny away to a room almost as soon as an Emergency doctor had examined him.

Nudger stood in the medicinal atmosphere of Emergency and looked around. There was a plump and busty redhead sitting at a counter with a sign on it that said ADMISSIONS. She was no priest and Nudger had nothing to admit to her. He tried to avoid her glance, but she'd noticed he was with Danny and beckoned him over with a smile and a wave. It wasn't the kind of invitation he could refuse.

When he leaned on the counter she looked at him with knowing green eyes and said, "Your friend doesn't seem to carry medical insurance."

Nudger sighed. "I'll co-sign for him." He wondered how long the thousand dollars Vanita Lane had given him would last at this rate.

The woman behind the counter asked myriad questions, keyed information into a computer, and made some entries on a form. Had Nudger sign the form. The hospital was now authorized to perform surgery on his bank account. The redhead thanked him, told him where he could wait for word about Danny, and began fastening papers together with a gigantic black stapler that made a grinding, metallic *crunch!* each time she brought the heel of her hand down on it.

Nudger sat in a molded plastic chair in the waiting room and listened to the stapler, then he read and reread a *Fortune* magazine for about an hour. He knew the federal discount rate was going to drop. Knew he should get out of stocks and into bonds. Had no stocks. Had no bonds. Still, these things were nice to know.

After a while a middle-aged man with black eyes and jet-black hair emerged from behind some wide, swinging doors and looked around. There was a weary and calm air about him. He locked gazes with Nudger and walked over to him. "You're Mr. Nudger?"

Nudger said he was. He stood up out of the hard plastic chair and dropped *Fortune* into it.

The man introduced himself as Dr. Rashnad. He had a high-pitched voice and an Indian accent, a reassuring smile.

Nudger waited for the reason for that reassurance.

"Your friend Daniel Evers is going to be fine, Mr. Nudger. We did a series of tests on him. His larynx is bruised and there's some cartilage damage in the neck area, but it will heal soon enough and return to normal. And tests indicate there was no damage due to decreased supply of oxygen to the brain, as there sometimes is in traumatic asphyxiation cases."

Nudger felt relief settle deep into him, as if he'd downed a slug of good scotch.

"We'll keep him overnight for observation," the doctor said. "He should be able to leave in the morning."

"Can I see him now?"

"Ah, of course. But he'll have difficulty talking. Don't engage him in unnecessary conversation, please." The doctor glanced at his watch. He had very delicate wrists and hands. "The nurse at the desk should know his room number by now. I must see another patient, Mr. Nudger."

Nudger thanked him and watched him walk away and push

through the wide swinging doors. Something white was stuck to the heel of one of his shoes, flashing with each step.

The redhead behind the admissions counter did magical things with her computer, then told Nudger that Danny was in Room 335.

On his way up in the elevator, he formulated the few questions he needed to ask Danny despite the doctor's advice. Made them yes-or-no questions, so all Danny had to do was nod.

Room 335 smelled like Listerine mouthwash. Danny didn't look bad. He was wearing a white hospital gown and was propped up on pillows. When he saw Nudger he managed a sad basset-hound grin. The red line was still visible across his throat, like an obscene necklace. There was a patch of white gauze and a strip of adhesive tape on the side of his neck where Nudger had used the knife to cut the twine, and some of Danny, to let Danny suck in some air. He was pulling more air into his lungs now.

He croaked as if he had a throat full of ground glass, "Thanks, Nudge."

"Don't try to talk," Nudger said. He dragged over a chair and sat down next to the bed. "Give me a nod or a shake of your head, though, okay?"

Danny nodded. The action made him swallow. His throat made a muted sound like small bones breaking beneath a blanket. Nudger felt a thrust of rage at Roger Bobinet and the skeleton. To make sure his anger wasn't misdirected he said, "A skinny guy or a handsome all-American type do this to you?"

Danny nodded. Held up two fingers. "Both," he croaked. "Skinny only watched. The other guy—looked like the fella used to play quarterback for the Dallas Cowboys—he was the one did the nasty work. He—"

Wait a minute. Nudger raised a hand. Said, "Just nod or shake your head, remember, Danny?"

Danny clamped his lips together and nodded.

"Did they say what they wanted?"

A nod. Danny pointed at Nudger. There was vanilla icing under his fingernail.

"They wanted to see me?"

Nod.

"They say what about?"

Danny shook his head no.

Nudger had to ask. "They seem angry at me?"

Danny managed to shrug beneath the ridiculous white gown.

"They just do that to you for kicks?" Nudger asked.

Danny pointed at Nudger again. "They said to tell you about it. Tell you they wanna talk to you." Danny gave a strangled cough and screwed up his face in agony.

Nudger said, "Goddammit, shut up, Danny!"

Danny appeared chastised. His somber brown eyes were misted from pain. Nudger couldn't look at him without his own eyes watering. He looked instead at the green plastic water pitcher on the tray next to the bed. "They leave any other kinda message?"

In his peripheral vision he saw Danny shake his head no.

Nudger stood up. He walked to the window and gazed outside. Traffic was streaming past on Clayton Road. The sun glanced off the roofs of passing cars, causing them to glitter like mobile jewels. It had to be hot out there. At least Danny's room was cool, even if it did smell like a bottle of mouthwash.

He looked down at Danny, who now had his eyes lightly closed. Maybe they'd given him a sedative. Painkiller.

"The doctor said you could go home in the morning," Nudger told him.

Danny nodded, not opening his eyes. Slipping away.

"You be okay if I leave now?" Nudger asked.

Danny nodded again, more feebly. He raised a hand about six inches off the bed, where it hung weightlessly for a few seconds, then dropped back to the mattress.

Nudger walked softly out of the room and closed the door behind him.

He was sure Danny was safe. If Bobinet and the skeleton had meant to kill him, he'd be dead. What they'd committed was a casual act of cruelty simply to keep Nudger frightened into obedience. What Bobinet had done to the canary and the dog, and maybe Ed Franks. But it would have been bad strategy to kill Danny and call the law's attention to Nudger so he might have to reveal his arrangement with the skeleton and Bobinet. He wouldn't be out there searching for the diamonds if that happened, so it was best to throttle the poor guy in the doughnut shop only halfway to death.

Nudger found a phone in the hospital lobby and called Hammersmith. He was told by Ellis, the Third District desk sergeant, that Hammersmith wasn't in his office. Nudger took a chance and called Ricardo's, a restaurant that was partly responsible for changing Hammersmith from a lean and handsome cop to his present overblown condition.

Ricardo himself answered the phone and said Hammersmith was at his usual table, enjoying the special.

When Hammersmith came to the phone he said, "You tore me away from a plate of spaghetti, Nudge." This conjured up a mental image that caused Nudger's stomach to twitch.

He said, "I just came from St. Mary's Hospital. Roger Bobinet roughed up Danny."

Hammersmith said, "Dammit! He okay?"

"More or less. I found him with a piece of twine looped around his neck. Same kinda twine used to hang Raggedy Ann."

"Huh?"

Nudger explained to him what he'd found at Marlou Dee's apartment.

"So where's Miss Dee?" Hammersmith asked.

No harm in telling Hammersmith. "Safely hidden at a motel in Hannibal. The fewer folks who know about it the better."

"Gotcha, Nudge. Count me as one of those you haven't told. Danny been released from the hospital yet?"

"They're keeping him till morning. For observation. I think he'll be okay; no permanent damage, according to the examining doctor."

"Danny say why Bobinet did a job on him?"

"Yeah. The skeleton and Bobinet came to see me. They were irritated when I wasn't in my office, so they went down to the doughnut shop and used Danny to leave me a sort of message."

"Some message. The bastards!"

"Coulda been worse," Nudger said. "Think of Franks."

"You're right. St. Mary's, you say?"

"Room Three-thirty-five."

"I'll drop by and see Danny. Maybe he'll want to file an assault complaint."

"Maybe Raggedy Ann will."

"Only doing my job, Nudge. You come up with any of those missing diamonds?"

"Not yet."

"Clue me in when you learn something."

"You know I will."

"Thanks, Nudge, you're a gem." Hammersmith hung up abruptly to get back to his spaghetti.

When Nudger returned to his office there was a message on his answering machine from the skeleton:

"Guess you know by now we was by to see you, asshole. (Gasp! Cough!) We'll be looking for you again. Better be where we can find you. Have a nice day."

Nudger slumped low in his swivel chair and stared at the wall. His stomach was roiling, so he got a couple of antacid tablets out of the top drawer and chewed on them. *We'll be looking for you again.*

A wave of cold fear passed through him as he replayed the message in his mind. An amazing amount of menace had been transmitted over the phone. The skeleton had reached out and touched him.

26

Nudger was waiting for Claudia when she got home from work. She took a step into the apartment, saw him sitting on the sofa, and her lean body stiffened for a moment in alarm. Then she smiled. She was wearing a summery lemon-colored blouse and matching slacks. Had on oversized white fake pearls that draped from her neck like small but lush tropical fruit. She was dressed cool but looked warm; there was a sheen of perspiration on her face and bare arms. Nudger figured she was too beautiful to sweat; she glistened.

Standing there glistening she said, "I got through the day okay. Didn't see any sign of the police, though."

"They were there," he assured her. "Way it works, you're not supposed to see them unless you need them."

She dropped her apparently heavy attaché case in the wing chair and swayed into the kitchen. He heard her clattering around in there, and a few minutes later she came out carrying two glasses of water with ice in them. She gave one of the clinking glasses to Nudger and sat down on the other end of the sofa. Crossed her legs and began slowly pumping one of them, the way women do.

He said, "I was looking out the window a few minutes ago and saw Larry Ervine drive past. He probably relieved whoever was watching over you today."

"I feel safe with him on the job," Claudia said. "So what time will *his* relief arrive? About midnight?"

"About. But in a case like this it wouldn't surprise me if Ervine caught some sleep after midnight and stayed in the area. He's that kinda cop. And he's still plenty sensitive about what happened to Ed Franks. Danny's another matter. That happened in Maplewood, just beyond the city line."

Claudia set her glass of water on a *Time* magazine lying on the table next to the sofa. She looked puzzled and alarmed. "Danny?"

Nudger told her what the skeleton and Roger Bobinet had done to Danny. He got mad again merely by talking about it.

"But he's all right?" she asked anxiously.

"He will be. He comes home from the hospital tomorrow."

"Bastards! Anybody who'd hurt someone like Danny . . . What about the doughnut shop?"

"I hung the CLOSED sign in the window. But if I know Danny he'll be behind the counter by tomorrow afternoon. Grease is in his blood."

"Will he be safe? I mean, what if this Bobinet psychopath comes back?"

"That's not likely," Nudger said. "And the Maplewood police will have the doughnut shop under surveillance. They'd like nothing more than to collar a couple of big-time killers and jewel thieves."

Claudia unbuttoned her blouse in a casual way that told Nudger she was merely trying to cool off, not heat up. She picked up her glass and sipped some ice water. Licked her lips and caressed the cool curve of the glass with lazy fingers.

Lounging gracefully with her bra showing, gleaming with perspiration and sipping a tall cool drink, she looked like a character out of a Tennessee Williams play. Every now and then, during long and sultry stretches of slowed time, Nudger thought of St. Louis as a southern and not a midwestern city. That was one of its schizophrenic sides: New Orleans north. Here and there you could order grits.

Nudger made himself stop staring at Claudia and excused himself to phone Marlou at Aunt Polly's.

No answer. She was out somewhere. Eating an early supper or going for a walk or buying a magazine, he hoped. Or gazing at her favorite riverboat. Something innocent like that, in the land of Tom and Huck. He hung up the phone.

"Your friend not home?" Claudia asked.

"Not right now." He gnawed on his lower lip, then ran a hand over the crown of his head where his hair was thinning. Pulled the hand away. Didn't want to feel that.

"Worried about her?" Claudia asked.

Nudger rested his fingertips on the phone again, then walked away from it. "More than she is, I guess."

He and Claudia took her car to Del Pietro's Restaurant over on Hampton. It gave Ervine something to do, but it made Nudger uneasy, sitting where Franks had sat. Could an economy car really be haunted?

They had pasta and the house red wine. Ervine sat at the bar drinking what looked like club soda and munching peanuts, occasionally glancing at Nudger and Claudia in the mirror. Living a cop's life. Loving it on one level, hating it on another. Nudger knew how it was.

When Nudger and Claudia were finished eating they drove to the Ted Drewes frozen custard stand on Chippewa and stood in line for a couple of chocolate chip concretes. Drewes's concretes were delicious custard concoctions so thick that before the kids working behind the counter handed them to customers, they turned the cups upside down to demonstrate that the contents wouldn't pour out.

Drewes was crowded, as it invariably was on warm summer nights. Native South St. Louisans ambling around in shorts and T-shirts and leaning on their pickup trucks, mixing with trendy types from West County, wearing designer clothes and lounging against their Porsches and Jaguars.

Like many customers, Nudger and Claudia sat in their car and leisurely worked on their concretes with plastic spoons. Ervine seemed to sense they were going to give him time to treat himself. Nudger saw him buy a huge chocolate sundae and carry it to his unmarked gray Plymouth parked in the row behind Nudger's car, eating as he walked.

Lightning was flashing in the west over St. Charles when Nudger dropped the empty waxed cups in a battered trash barrel and drove from the parking lot. It might simply be chain lightning, the kind that didn't preclude rain. Or the illuminated sky might be the precursor of a violent summer thunderstorm. Unpredictable weather blew in from the west this time of year. Sometimes tornadoes. No point checking with the folks at the Weather Bureau, though, or one of the talking-suit meteorologists on TV news; summers in St. Louis, Nudger's guess was as good as theirs.

A brisk wind had kicked up and was driving dust and zoysia grass cuttings along Claudia's street when Nudger parked the car. It had cooled off and they'd driven home with the windows down. Claudia stood on the sidewalk while he cranked the glass back up. Then he climbed out of the car and locked it. He held her arm and kept looking around continually, like a fighter pilot patrolling over enemy territory, as they walked along the sidewalk to her building.

He felt better when they were inside and he'd looked through the apartment. They were alone, and everything seemed to be as they'd left it. No bogeymen seeking stolen diamonds. He nodded to Claudia standing by the door and she set the locks.

It had suddenly gotten dark outside except for frequent flashes of lightning. Thunder rolled in from the west like low-level cannon fire, rumbling and cracking in the bent gray sky above the apartment.

Claudia walked in her elegant way across the room and switched on a lamp. It sent a soft yellow glow over everything.

The wind tossed a sheet of rain against the front windows, rattling the panes then dying to a watery whisper.

She glanced in the direction of the noise and said, "It's dark, Nudger, but it's still early. What'll we do till bedtime?"

He said, "I've got an idea."

Half awake, dreaming in waves, he lay on his back in the dark and felt again the warm, strong softness of Claudia's eager body. Then he was flying. Soaring higher and higher in tightening arcs while she moaned in his ear. She screamed.

He opened his eyes.

Huh? Not Claudia screaming. Someone else.

Something else.

Sirens.

The erection he'd awakened with shrank from body and consciousness as his dream faded. For a few seconds he lay listening. He was nude. Perspiring. The sheet was damp beneath him. The room was warm and still smelled of sex. Rain was no longer falling—not hard enough for him to hear, anyway—but occasional flashes of brilliance popped soundlessly in the night sky, like celestial flashbulbs illuminating the city. The sirens were getting louder.

He rotated his wrist to look at the luminous hands of his watch, then remembered he'd removed it last night. Hadn't wanted to scratch Claudia.

He groped around on the table by the bed. *Ouch!* Bent back a fingernail on the clock radio. He found the watch and looked at it. Christ! One o'clock.

A new sound. Someone pounding on the back door that led from the kitchen to the rear steps and fire escape.

Claudia awoke and sat bolt upright beside him. Lightning flashed, and he saw her in bold outline, nude and rigid, reminding him of that movie scene when the bride of Frankenstein is jolted to life by electricity.

"Jesus!" she said. "What's that, Nudger?"

"Oh, just sirens, lightning, somebody beating on the door."

He struggled up out of the bed and wrestled into his pants. Almost lost his balance and fell. He wound up facing the window and realized some of what he'd assumed was lightning carried alternating blue and red hues. Revolving roofbar lights of police cars.

He said, "Stay here," to Claudia and padded barefoot through the dancing light toward the kitchen.

The pounding on the door got louder and took on more urgency as he got closer.

Even the tile floor in the kitchen was warm beneath his bare feet, but he hardly noticed. He pulled aside the curtain on the back door's tiny window. A dim light was burning in the landing, and Nudger felt a stab of fear before he recognized that the face just a few inches from his own on the other side of the glass belonged to Larry Ervine.

"Open up, Nudge!"

Nudger fumbled the chain lock loose, threw the bolt on the lock beneath it, and opened the door.

"What the hell's going down, Larry?"

When Ervine started to speak, Nudger realized he was breathing hard. "Milner, the guy watching the back of the building, saw somebody climbing the fire escape. Whoever it was stopped at the window right there." Ervine motioned with his head toward the window on the landing, directly opposite Claudia's back door. "Milner tried to get up close, but the man on the fire escape saw him and had time to climb down low enough to jump to the ground. Took off running toward Grand Avenue. Milner radioed for help and chased the guy but the sonuvabitch could run like Bambi."

"Bobinet?" Nudger asked.

"Yeah, who else? Milner said he was about medium size and had to be relatively young, way he could scat. Anyways, a patrol car on the way to the scene spots him on Grand and hits the siren and lights. Uniforms figure they got him. Guy stops running, all right. But he turns around and opens up on the car with something big. Magnum probably. Blew the windshield out and sent another slug through the radiator, water pump, and an oil line; a challenge for Mr. Goodwrench."

"Anybody get hit?"

"Nope, just the car. One of the uniforms chased Bobinet—or whoever it was—south on Grand but lost him. Got off a couple of shots at him but missed. You know how it is, you run flat out and stop and plant your feet to fire your gun, you're puffin' and shakin' like a train about to pull outa the station. How the hell you gonna hit anything that way?"

"Bobinet managed some good shooting."

"Yeah, didn't he, though?"

Nudger drew a deep breath as he noticed Ervine was looking beyond him into the kitchen. He turned and saw Claudia in her blue terry cloth robe, its sash yanked tight around her slender waist. Her bare toes were curled tight against the tile floor. She'd been standing there listening.

"You don't mind, ma'am," Ervine said, "I'd like to leave a couple of men here while I take Nudger a few blocks away so he can see what's happenin'."

Claudia looked at Nudger. Fear glinted in her dark eyes. And something else. She was angry.

He wanted to stay with her, but he knew she'd be under guard and safe. "It'll be okay," he told her. "I'll be back soon."

She shrugged and turned away.

Ervine motioned with his hand and there was a lot of clomping on the stairs.

A uniform and a plainclothes cop barged in, big men who made the kitchen and Claudia look small. Claudia seemed to gain assurance from their overwhelming bulk.

"This is Davis and . . ." Ervine looked at the uniform.

"Humphreys," the uniform said. He was in his thirties but had one of those faces that made him look nineteen at a glance. Nudger noticed the flap on his black leather holster was unsnapped. Bobinet had unnerved the troops.

Davis and Humphreys nodded to Claudia, who said, "Want

some coffee?" What else did you say to two brontosaurus-size cops in your kitchen?

Ervine rested a hand on Nudger's shoulder, guiding him out onto the dim landing. Nudger heard the door locks snick behind them as he followed Ervine down the narrow steps to the building's back door.

The cruiser was angled with a front wheel up on the curb. As they walked toward it Nudger saw the glitter of glass around and behind it from the shot-out windshield. Three other cruisers were parked nearby. Also a couple of unmarked cars. About a dozen uniforms and cops in street clothes were milling around. Some looked bored. Others looked apprehensive.

Ervine touched Nudger's elbow and stopped him when they were about twenty feet from the car. The tire that had jumped the curb was completely deflated and wrapped around the rim. Nudger could smell gasoline and hot oil now. He saw a dark puddle beneath the front of the car. One of the uniforms raised the hood. Another bent over with a fire extinguisher and began methodically spraying foam into the engine compartment. The extinguisher was making a soft hissing sound.

A cop nearby was standing off by himself, dabbing at a cut on his cheek with a white handkerchief. Apparently that was the only injury, a minor nick, probably from flying glass. Nudger hoped the two uniforms who'd been in the car knew how lucky they were not to have gotten closer before Bobinet opened fire.

Ervine looked hard at Nudger and said, "I wanted to get you away so's we could talk outa earshot of your Miss Bettencourt. You think our guy knew you were staying overnight in her apartment?"

Nudger said, "Probably. It's the kinda thing he'd know."

"That's what I figured. He musta realized the place was being watched, even at one in the morning, but still he tried to get inside."

"I'm not surprised," Nudger said. "Bobinet's got the ego for it. Probably enjoyed the challenge of trying to get past you the back way."

"Some balls," Ervine said. "Badman with a set like that's liable to do any fuckin' thing."

"It's proving out that way," Nudger said. He watched as a tow truck with a flashing yellow roof light rolled slowly down Grand toward the crippled police car. A heavy chain was clanking rhythmically against its steel boom. "Bobinet and the skeleton tried to get in touch with me earlier today. Beat up a friend of mine. Damn near choked him to death."

"I heard," Ervine said. "Danny something. Fella runs a doughnut shop."

"Well, after they worked him over they told him they were looking for me."

"Any idea what they want?"

"Not exactly."

An unmarked Pontiac pulled to the curb beyond where the tow truck was backing toward the damaged car. It sat idling for a moment with its taillights bright red; the driver still had his foot on the brake pedal. Then the lights winked out and exhaust stopped trailing from the car's tailpipe.

Hammersmith climbed out, looked around, and saw Nudger and Ervine. He walked toward them. When he got close, Nudger saw his gray hair was tousled and his eyes were puffy. Hammersmith didn't look his usual obese yet sleek self. He nodded to Nudger and Ervine. "Claudia okay?" he asked.

"Yes, sir," Ervine said. "She's fine."

Hammersmith kept looking at Ervine. "Well?"

Ervine told him what had happened, speaking bureaucratese but not wasting a word. A veteran cop. He made the night seem dull.

Hammersmith glanced at the damaged squad car being winched up so its front wheels cleared the pavement. Clumps of dirt dropped from its undercarriage, making even more of a mess on the street. After firing up a cigar, Hammersmith gazed over its glowing ember at Nudger. "This Bobinet's a grade-A desperado, Nudge. He made me get outa bed. I want the bastard."

Ervine said, "He must wanna see Nudger in the worst possible way."

Hammersmith flicked ashes in a fiery cascade to the sidewalk. "Yeah. And for the worst possible reason."

27

Nudger was able to get another few hours of sleep before Claudia shook him awake.

She was standing over him fully dressed. Her right hand was on his shoulder and a thin gold chain with a cubic zirconia stone was dangling from her neck, inches from his face. The mock diamond was realistic enough to shoot points of light like darts into his eyes as the stone jiggled on the chain each time Claudia shook him. ". . . Up, Nudger. You want to get up?"

"Humph? Why should I want that?"

"It's almost eight o'clock. I'm leaving for work."

Nudger rubbed his eyes. Scooted backward so his head was propped against the headboard. Squinted. "There's daylight outside," he said.

She smiled. "Been that way a few hours."

He stared up at her. She was beautiful but there were fine lines of strain in her lean face. The faint sweet scent of her perfume drifted down to him. Flower of life. *Wake up, Nudger.* He said, "You get back to sleep last night?"

"No," she admitted. "I lay there with my eyes open and kept hearing faint sounds. Like someone trying to get in. I almost woke you up a few times."

"You should have."

"No real reason. After what happened, I knew my imagination was in high gear. Anyway, you needed your sleep. Still do. I wouldn't have woke you just now, only you have to leave soon to pick up Danny at the hospital."

"Yeah," Nudger said. "If I don't get him out of there by ten o'clock they remove one of his vital organs and charge for another day."

She kissed his forehead. Her lips were cool. The equally cool chain and stone brushed his nose. "I've gotta get out of here, Nudger. Coffee's made."

He'd known she'd made coffee; he'd smelled it beyond the whiff of perfume.

She let her fingertips walk over his shoulder, then her legs walked her toward the door. He watched the lazy switch of her hips.

"Be extra careful," Nudger said. "This is real."

"I realized that," she said, "when I found the corpse in my car."

She left the bedroom. He heard her high heels tap across the hardwood floor, go quiet as she crossed the carpet, *Tap! Tap!* again on wood. The apartment door opened and closed. She slammed it twice, making sure it was locked behind her.

Nudger dragged himself up to slump on the edge of the mattress. He ran his tongue around dry teeth and gums. Tasted foul. So foul it prompted him to stand up and trudge into the bathroom, where he brushed his teeth first thing and then used some kind of green mouthwash Claudia had bought. The label had an illustration of surf breaking over pine trees.

After showering and dressing, he poured a cup of coffee and sat at the kitchen table with it, waiting for his toast to pop up. He turned on the radio and listened to the news while the coffee taste mingled with the strong minty aftermath of the mouthwash.

One of the lead stories was about the prowler in South St. Louis who'd been pursued by police and escaped when he'd shot and disabled a patrol car, slightly injuring one officer. No mention was made of who the prowler might have been, or even where specifically he'd been prowling. Hammersmith, or maybe Springer, holding cards close to the vest.

The toast popped up and stood at attention, emitting parallel curls of smoke. Nudger yanked both pieces out and away from the toaster and examined them to see how badly they were burned. He decided they were about twenty percent edible. Enough.

He broke off inedible portions, then scraped the charred surfaces with a knife. Spread strawberry jam over what was left and sat staring at it. He decided there wasn't enough to bother with after all and deposited it in the sink and ran the garbage disposal.

He finished his coffee, then had a second cup to keep his heart pumping and his bodily fluids circulating. Then he switched off the radio, wiped crumbs from the table, and turned off the burner under the coffeepot.

He left the apartment to go and reclaim Danny from the hospital, still tasting mint.

It wasn't all that difficult. Nudger signed this, signed that, and Danny was escorted by a young volunteer nurses' aide to the lobby and exit. Which officially kept him under medical care until he walked outside into the summer heat, where, if he keeled over, the entire process of admission, treatment, and release would start over. The smiling young aide had handed Nudger a large rolled-up foam rubber pad with points all over it. "Mr. Evers can take this home," she'd said, as if it were something of hers he'd long admired.

Nudger hugged the bulky roll of blue foam rubber to him. It had about it the size and unwieldiness of a misshapen beach ball. "What is it?"

"Special mattress pad," Danny said. He was still hoarse, but he didn't seem to be in any pain. "Really great for the back, Nudge. You oughta try one."

Nudger thought he and a hospital might be in each other's futures, the way things were going.

He made sure Danny was comfortable in the front seat of the Granada, then opened the trunk and stuffed the mass of blue foam rubber inside. Gave it an experimental prod with a fingertip. All those little rubber points, like a training mattress for an Indian fakir trying to work his way up to a bed of nails. It didn't look or feel comfortable to Nudger, but who could tell? He slammed the trunk lid closed, then walked around the car and slid in behind the steering wheel.

"Making it okay?" he asked Danny.

"I feel all right, Nudge. Weak, is all. And my throat's still sore from where that psycho tried to choke me."

"You're lucky you're still alive," Nudger told him.

Danny nodded slowly, as if he wasn't so sure. Maybe he felt worse than he was letting on. He said, "Let's head for the doughnut shop, Nudge."

"Let's head for your apartment," Nudger told him. "You go back to hoisting Dunker Delites too soon and you might have a relapse." *Might even hurt your back and really need that blue pad.*

"Nudge—"

"Bullshit, Danny! Do yourself a favor and leave the place closed for the day. What business you gonna lose? Your only regular customers are from the neighborhood; what are they gonna do, drive six miles to Dunkin Donuts?"

Danny stared out the windshield for a while. "Well, maybe I can get Ray to man the shop. Just for today."

Danny's incredibly lazy cousin Ray subsisted on various kinds of government payments and welfare in the St. James Apartments, where Danny now lived, not far west on Manchester from the doughnut shop.

"Last time Ray tried to bake," Nudger reminded him, "the fire department had to get in on the act." Ever since Danny had moved into the St. James complex, Ray had been a pain in the ass, sponging off him and getting fat on leftover pastry. "Keep the place locked up for the day, Danny. Save yourself having to clean up after Ray. And your regular customers'll understand."

Danny settled back in the seat and closed his eyes. "I suppose you're right, Nudge," he said in a hoarse whisper. "Probably take another day before my throat stops aching. Hey, you mind stopping by Walgreen's Drugstore so I can get a prescription for pain pills filled?"

"Not at all," Nudger said. "Now you're being reasonable."

"Well, I appreciate what you done for me, Nudge. Least I can do is follow your advice."

"The least," Nudger said.

"You had breakfast yet?"

"Why? Didn't they feed you in the hospital?"

"No. They knew I was checking out."

"Wanna stop someplace? Get some eggs or hotcakes down you?"

"I don't think so, Nudge. I don't feel quite up to that. What I had in mind, we could brew some coffee at my place. Have that and some Dunker Delites."

"Last time you made a batch of Dunker Delites was yesterday morning," Nudger said.

"I could microwave 'em. How 'bout it, Nudge?"

"I guess not this morning," Nudger said. "I already had toast."

After getting Danny settled in his apartment, Nudger walked over to Ray's, stood in the late morning sun, and rang the doorbell.

Ray hadn't gotten out of bed yet today. He was wearing a ridiculously tight white undershirt and baggy gray boxer shorts, with a pattern of red, fork-tailed devils on them, when he opened the door. He scratched his head, yawned, and glared at Nudger. "Whaddaya want?"

Nudger explained what had happened and asked him to look

in on Danny every few hours, noticing that the devils were each wielding a spear with a fancy point shaped like a woman. He wondered what Freud would have made of that.

Ray said, "Sure. Now disappear." He scratched his crotch, yawned again, then shut the door.

He was no disciple of Miss Manners unless he wanted something.

Nudger knew Ray was returning to bed, so he leaned on the doorbell for at least a minute before turning and walking back to his car.

The apartment door remained closed as Nudger drove away, but he figured he'd made it impossible for Ray to go back to sleep.

He felt good about that.

28

The digital readout on Nudger's answering machine told him he had three messages. He sat in the breeze of the air conditioner and waited for the office to cool off, knowing the kind of messages he'd be likely to receive would tend to generate heat of their own; better to wait before hearing them.

He stood up, paced to the window, and looked outside for the Maplewood police car he'd noticed as he was coming into the building. The white patrol car with the maple-leaf seal on its door was still parked half a block down Manchester. Nice to see. At least a measure of protection.

Nudger could put it off no longer. He finally slumped back down in his swivel chair, rolled up his sleeves, and punched the Play button on the machine.

The first message was from Eileen. Soon as he recognized her voice, he fast-forwarded to the second message. All the recorded Eileen got out was "Nudger, I—"

Message number two was short and simple: a request to call New York City detective Rico Stompano.

Nudger decided to return Stompano's call before listening

to the third message. He rummaged through the clutter on his desk until he found the slip of paper on which was scrawled Stompano's number. Dialed direct.

He was put on hold. Thank God there was no Muzak.

A nasal East Coast voice said, "Nudger?"

"Still waiting," Nudger said.

"This is Rico Stompano. Thought you oughta know something. Guy named Norville Coates gave us a call yesterday. He's a bellhop at the Meridian Hotel. Turns out he's in charge of gathering the hotel's outgoing mail and transporting it to the post office each day."

Eeek! Nudger sat up straighter in his swivel chair.

Stompano continued. "Seems our friend Norville was in the habit of opening the supposedly sealed mail sack and examining interesting-looking parcels the guests mailed at the hotel, setting them aside so he could get into them later. If it looked like the package could be opened and resealed, he'd go through the contents and remove anything valuable. Then he'd put the package back together and send it out, more or less the way it had been, with the next day's mail."

"An industrious kinda guy."

"But no rarity. We got hustlers up the ass in this city."

Nudger was sure he knew where the conversation was going. "Then Winslow *did* mail the diamonds."

"Sure. But don't step out ahead of yourself, Nudger, or you might get run over by some fuckhead looks familiar. Norville had set aside Winslow's package with a few others and was going to break into them in the wee hours when he was on the night shift. But when Winslow's body was found, Norville got the chills and didn't wanna play any part in a murder investigation. Also didn't want his dips into the mailbag to come to light while said murder was being looked into. So he dropped everything with a stamp on it into the mailbox outside the hotel. Then, when we questioned him, he played dumb."

"So why's he talking now?" Nudger asked.

"Fingerprints."

"Huh?"

"Friend Norville didn't know we could lift fingerprints off wrapping paper. When he got worried and did a little research and found it was possible, he thought as soon as the Winslow package turned up in the investigation, his prints would be lifted from it and he might be nailed for the murder. Wanted to get a lawyer and set the record straight before that happened. All of a sudden tampering with the mail didn't seem so serious."

"He remember the address on the package?"

"Says he doesn't. I believe him. Guy's got an IQ in the minus range. Also, he had no interest in where the packages were headed, only what was in them he might be able to steal and sell. Norville's got himself a drug habit needs constant feeding."

"And he was inches away from a million dollars in diamonds," Nudger said.

Stompano laughed. "He just found out about that. He keeps mumbling he played everything wrong. I keep reminding him an obstruction of justice charge and mail tampering's better'n Murder One."

Nudger said, "How'd he describe the package?"

"About the size of a shoebox only longer—that was what attracted his attention, the odd size. Not very heavy, as he recalls, and didn't rattle when he shook it. Wrapped in plain brown paper, tied with string or twine, and plastered with stamps. He thinks it was addressed with a black felt-tip pen. Printed right on the paper, no label. Says he doesn't recall even one letter of the name or address."

"I'll bet."

"Well, can't expect a guy like Norville to come completely clean. He wouldn't know himself when he looked in the mirror."

"How much space does a million in diamonds take up?" Nudger asked.

"Hell, that's no more'n a handful of rocks, Nudger. In this case, anyway, because of the high quality of the diamonds. But you'd ship it carefully. You don't mail that kinda thing without plenty of packing around it, so it'll stand up to any sorta beating the postal service gives it and not spill out on the floor."

"Think the diamonds were in the package?" Nudger asked.

Stompano didn't hesitate. "That's my guess. Either that or souvenir Hard Rock Cafe T-shirts."

"You notify the St. Louis police about this?"

Stompano chuckled. "Notified them first thing, Nudger. Whaddya think, you're Double-Oh-Seven or some such shit, like we're gonna clue you in on secret information?"

"Don't get testy," Nudger said.

"How us New Yorkers are. Wouldn't tell you how to get to fucking Carnegie Hall, either. Other hand, I *did* try to get in touch with you and let you know about this development."

"You got a point," Nudger admitted. "I owe you."

"Owe me to who?" Stompano asked.

Nudger said, "Can't get ahead of you East Coasters." But Stompano had hung up.

Nudger let the receiver clatter into its cradle. He leaned back in his chair, not even hearing it squeal. He was seeing again the brown twine looped around Danny's neck. Thinking of how Norville Coates had described the package Winslow tried to mail before his death. He played again in his mind what Stompano had said about how much space the diamonds would take up. A handful of diamonds and padding. What kind of padding? Kleenexes? Wadded newspaper? A folded shirt? If the package broke open in the course of its journey through the machinery of the postal service, would the diamonds be safe from discovery packed that way?

Then another question wedged its way into Nudger's mind. Would Winslow want the recipient of the package to *realize* it contained stolen diamonds?

Looked at in that light, what was stalking the dark regions of his subconscious became discernible. Seemed possible.

He stood up, switched off the air conditioner, and was about to walk from the office when he remembered the third message on his machine.

This one was from the skeleton, telling Nudger they needed

to talk and commanding him to stay in his office and wait for another phone call. "Stay by that phone like a goddamn debutante waiting for an invitation to the ball," said the skeleton's reedy, recorded voice. *Cough! Wheeze.*

Nudger erased all his messages, reset the machine, and left the office.

He drove to Marlou Dee's apartment.

It was exactly the way he'd left it. The way the skeleton and Roger Bobinet had left it after their search-and-destroy mission. Nudger stood just inside the door and listened to the humming silence, breathed the hot, stale air, strained to listen even more intently. From the apartment below, the prattle of a TV tuned too loud to an inane game show filtered up through the floor like mutterings from hell.

Nudger willed his heartbeat to slow. He popped an antacid tablet into his mouth and chewed it as he walked toward the bedroom. *Whump! Whump!* went his heart.

Raggedy Ann was still dangling from the light fixture, the thick brown twine tight around her pathetic cloth neck. As Nudger recalled, each Raggedy Ann had a red heart drawn or sewn on its chest beneath its dress. A saleswoman had informed him of this when he'd bought such a doll for the daughter of a woman he'd briefly dated last year when he and Claudia were on the outs.

Feeling like some kind of goulish pervert, he stepped close to the hanged doll and raised its cloth dress.

Open-heart surgery had been performed on Raggedy Ann. Not very well, as the heart hadn't been replaced. Beneath the dress was a gaping hole in the chest, from which several gray wisps of stuffing bulged.

Nudger tried to untie the knot around the doll's neck, but it was too tight. He looked around and noticed a pair of manicure scissors lying in the mess on the floor. Perfect for twine and toenails. With some difficulty, he cut the twine.

He examined Raggedy Ann more closely.

The chest cavity would easily accommodate a handful of diamonds.

Dr. Nudger probed around with a fingertip, conducting the postmortem.

If poor Raggedy Ann had contained diamonds, they'd all been removed during surgery. Like gallstones that glittered. It was unlikely the skeleton and Bobinet had performed the operation, or they wouldn't still be running after the diamonds.

Nudger understood now why Danny had been choked with an identical length of coarse brown twine. Why the skeleton and Bobinet were looking for him. They must have found the doll with the hollowed-out chest. And probably the wrapping paper, with its New York postmark, and twine in Marlou's trash.

They knew now that the diamonds had been mailed to St. Louis. Knew somebody had found them in the doll before they'd had a chance to get to them. They were mad about that—so much so that sadistic Bobinet had played out a lynching on innocent courier Raggedy Ann. Almost done the same with Danny. Now they were looking for Nudger to tell him the diamonds had been sent to Marlou's address. To ask him where Marlou was.

Nudger stood for a moment in the center of the littered bedroom, absently holding Raggedy Ann close to him as if she were a real and abused child. Until all of a sudden he pictured himself, a grown man needing a shave and hugging a doll. There was an image to undermine machismo.

Holding the doll at his side in a more manly fashion, as if it were a chain saw, he hurried out into the heat. He got in the Granada and aimed it north toward Hannibal, not noticing the drab gray rental car that followed.

29

Nudger stood in the shade of the motel catwalk and knocked on the door to Marlou's room, feeling the lowering evening sun hot on the backs of his knees. He listened to the shouting and laughing of kids splashing around in the swimming pool behind him. The scent of honeysuckle growing on a trellis alongside the building drifted to him on the warm breeze. Summertime.

He knocked again.

No answer. No sound from the other side of the door.

He turned around and watched a chubby teenage boy do a cannonball off the diving board. The splash exploded like a thunderclap, and glittering drops of water arced through the air and stained the pale concrete close to Nudger. The kid bobbed to the still-churning surface grinning and shaking water from his long hair. Nudger wondered what it would be like to be that young again and do something with such total abandon and joy.

He tried Marlou's door and found it locked, so he walked over to the motel office.

The elderly woman he thought of as Aunt Polly was seated

on a high stool behind the registration desk, reading a magazine about quilting. Nudger asked her if she knew where Miss Thatcher of Room 335 was.

"A young lady walked past the window about an hour ago," Aunt Polly said, lowering the magazine and peering at Nudger over her glasses. "Takes lotsa walks, that one. She some kinda exercise bug?"

"She gets bored easy."

"Well, maybe she went over on Main Street, to that buncha antique and souvenir shops. Find out all you wanna know about Samuel Clemens over there. Him and Mark Twain's one and the same."

Nudger smiled and said, "I know all I want to about him for now, but I'll try the shops."

"Walk straight down the drive and turn right," Aunt Polly said. "Then walk some more. Want me to tell her you was here if she comes back? Case you don't find her?"

"Yeah, thanks," Nudger said. He opened the office door and stepped outside into the heat. Heard the crisp snap of a page turning as he shut the door. How much could be written about quilting?

Despite Aunt Polly's advice, he decided to drive instead of walk. He got in the Granada and twisted the ignition key. Turned on the air conditioner. Raggedy Ann slumped beside him on the seat, grinning with inane happiness despite the ghastly fatal wound beneath her dress. He drove down the motel driveway and turned right toward the heart of Hannibal.

Main Street was sunny and thronging with tourists on the lookout for antiques or Mark Twain souvenirs. Nudger cruised the five blocks or so of the business district but saw no sign of Marlou. He strayed a little farther away and passed the leaning white frame house where Twain had lived. The hill where Huck and Tom supposedly had played. Well, at least the hill Twain had used as the model for the hill in his fiction. Maybe.

Still no sign of Marlou. Nudger supposed he'd have to park the car and start looking inside the shops and restaurants.

He drove down rustic Center Street and found a parking

space near the river. As he climbed out of the car he could see the riverboat that so enthused Marlou. The *Mark Twain* (what else?) was a large stern-wheeler, its windowed white decks rising like layers of a wedding cake. There was something Victorian and elegant about riverboats; Nudger could see why Marlou was intrigued. Maybe he'd make good on his promise to take her on the boat, if there was a cruise at a convenient time. If he ever found her.

He walked about fifty feet to his right so he could see the sign near the boat's gangplank. It said the next cruise left the dock at six-thirty, in a little over an hour. Maybe he and Marlou could be on it.

When he turned around, there she was. Standing by the Granada with her hands propped on her hips, staring at him.

He walked toward her. She was wearing tight, faded Levi's and a black T-shirt with a picture of Mark Twain over her nubby breasts. On her head rested a souvenir straw hat with a wide brim and a bright yellow ribbon on it. She was carrying what looked like a new straw purse that matched the hat. As Nudger approached she gave him her wide, country smile. Might have been the genuine Becky Thatcher.

"Want a strand of grass for between your teeth?" he asked.

Her grin turned inquisitive. "Huh?"

"Nothing. I've been looking for you."

"Been right here, more or less," she said. "Walking along the river. I like it down here. Seen the car from up near the grain towers and figured it might be yours. Came on down and knew it was. Old home day or something?"

"Old home day?"

"I mean, I'm pretty positive I saw that insurance fella, Stockton, up on Main Street. Looked again, though, and he was gone."

Nudger stared at her. "Bill Stockton, of Sloan Trust?"

"Yep. Same Bill Stockton that came around and questioned me right after Vanita died."

"What was he doing when you saw him?"

"Looking in a window at some antique dishes. On the other

side of the street from where I was, and down a ways. Didn't seem the type that'd be interested in old china."

"Not unless it was stolen and insured. Sure it was him?"

"Reasonably so. Hey!"

"Huh?"

She was staring inside the car. "Whatcha doin' with my Raggedy Ann in there?"

"I found it hanged from your bedroom chandelier with a piece of twine."

She swallowed hard, her Adam's apple working above the neck of the black T-shirt. Twain's nose was exactly over the jutting point of her right breast; gave him a certain dimension. "I mean, like, what'd you do, cut her down so you could bring her to me?"

"Sort of," Nudger said. "Something about her I wanna show you."

He opened the Granada's passenger-side door, leaned in, and straightened up holding the doll.

Marlou was already reaching for it. Nudger handed it over. "Notice anything different about it?"

"Sure, where those mean bastards tied string around her neck." Marlou's fingers began to massage the cloth doll's neck gently, as if to comfort it. Then her green eyes widened in puzzlement. Her fingers probed lower. She raised the doll's dress. Seemed for a moment as if she might cry. "God, what'd they do *that* to her for?"

"You don't know?"

She stared at him. Tears in her eyes. Acting? "'Course I don't know. Do you?"

"They went through your trash," Nudger said. "Found the wrapping paper and twine from the package. Figured out, when they found the doll like that, what had been in the package. But they weren't the ones who opened up the doll and removed the diamonds, or they wouldn't still be looking for them."

Marlou's mouth was gaping. "Wait a minute. You saying the diamonds was inside Raggedy Ann?"

"That's how Winslow hid and protected them when he mailed them from New York."

"I thought he didn't mail nothing."

"That's what everyone thought. The New York police found out later that he'd mailed a package. Had to have been the doll and the diamonds."

She shook her head from side to side so her red hair bounced. "Couldn't have been, Mr. Nudger."

He was already convinced by her reaction that she hadn't known the diamonds were in the doll. What kind of crap was she about to throw into the game now?

"Why not?" he asked.

"Heck, I had Raggedy Ann here since I was, like, nine years old."

Nudger leaned back against the car. Crossed his arms and stared out at the great brown river sliding past. Water rolling like time.

"Hear what I said, Mr. Nudger?"

"Sure did," Nudger said. "I'm thinking. Gotta do a lot of that in my business."

The diamonds had to have been in the doll, or why would its poor cloth heart have been so methodically ripped out? Someone had felt the doll, encountered the hardness of the diamonds, and performed doll surgery.

But suppose the diamonds had been mailed to someone else in St. Louis. And the someone who'd received them had hidden them in the Raggedy Ann doll without Marlou knowing about it.

Probably the only one who'd had the opportunity to do that was Marlou's sister, Vanita. Even though it put Marlou in a dangerous spot. Maybe the sisters hadn't gotten along as well as either of them pretended. Maybe neither of them was quite what she presented to the world. Deviousness could run in families.

Nudger thought about that supposed sequence of events. It was possible. Even likely. What safer place for Vanita to hide the diamonds after Winslow had sent them to her? And the theory would explain why, even under torture, Vanita hadn't told Roger Bobinet and the skeleton where the diamonds were hidden. She'd known their next victim would have been her baby sister. Blood thicker than water. Stronger than pain. Vanita finally being true and finding honor in the face of death.

Feeling slightly nauseated, Nudger used his palm to wipe sweat from his face.

Marlou said, "Got anything figured out yet, Mr. Nudger?"

A sole scraped a paving stone behind Nudger. Two long shadows fell on either side of him. "Yeah, Mr. Nudger," the wheezing voice of the skeleton said. "Do tell us if you got any answers."

"Figure this out fast," Roger Bobinet said, flashing his cereal-box smile. "I got my hand on a gun in my pocket. Wouldn't mind using it."

"Though you'd prefer a knife," Nudger said. His voice was high with fear. At least it hadn't cracked, turning him into a panicky adolescent.

Bobinet shrugged. "We don't get everything we prefer in this world, Nudger. Not right away. That's what this is all about." He grinned at Marlou. "Been looking forward to meeting you, sweetheart. I was a friend of your sister."

Amazingly, Marlou seemed unafraid. All three men stared at her when she said, "These the goons killed Raggedy Ann?"

30

"These are also the goons that killed your sister," Nudger reminded Marlou.

That fact seemed to have temporarily escaped her. She still appeared more enraged than afraid. Her green eyes narrowed and her freckles were almost lost in the red and mottled complexion of heightened blood pressure. She drew back a fist to strike at Bobinet, who grinned, caught the force of the blow with his palm, and jerked Marlou to the side so her momentum carried her past him and she almost fell.

"Little cunt's got some guts," the skeleton said. "But then so'd her sister." He wheezed. Coughed. "Fuckin' country air."

"That's what lung cancer'll do for you," Bobinet said, still watching Marlou. When he was sure she wasn't going anywhere, he turned toward Nudger, squinting against the low angled rays of the setting sun. "You see, Nudger, my pal here used to be a three-pack-a-day smoker, and he ain't got that much longer to enjoy his hard-earned riches. So we want the diamonds and we'll do what needs doing to get them. He's got nothing much left to lose, and I always lived as if I didn't."

The skeleton didn't change expression. "I ain't dead yet," he said. "Keeping in mind the gun I'm holding in *my* pocket, let's all of us walk over and get in that car." He motioned with his head toward a rented subcompact, a gray Ford Escort.

Bobinet led the way. Nudger and Marlou followed, Marlou clutching her Raggedy Ann doll. The skeleton followed with the gun, breathing hard, huffing like a locomotive pushing a train.

Nudger and the skeleton wedged themselves into the tiny backseat. Bobinet squeezed himself in behind the little car's steering wheel. Marlou sat beside him in front. The inside of the car was warm, and the skeleton smelled as sick as he was. There didn't seem to be enough air. For a while the only sound was that of the skeleton's labored breathing.

Bobinet half turned to face Marlou, and so he could see Nudger. "Now, we talk. We ask, first of all, Marcy Lou, where are the diamonds?"

Marlou glared at him. "Got no diamonds."

Bobinet smiled at her and shook his head slowly. "You, your sister, and Rupert fucking Winslow were in it together. We found the brown wrapping paper and twine, saw the New York postmark on it, in your apartment. Right near the bottom of the kitchen wastebasket. Found the doll the diamonds were stashed in. Know the weight of the doll and the diamonds together'd be just about what the postage was on the package." He leaned closer to her, handsome guy looking like he was about to do a Hollywood love scene with a starlet. Young romantics parked in lover's lane. "Marcy Lou, you got the diamonds, and before I'm done with you you'll goddamn beg to tell me where they are."

"If you found brown wrapping paper and twine in my apartment, somebody put it there. Not me. I never got a thing in the mail from New York City. Don't know anybody there and, like, I don't wanna."

Bobinet shifted his gaze to the backseat. "Whadda you say, Nudger?"

"Oh, I believe her."

"Couple of lying assholes, all right," the skeleton said. He had the gun out now where they could see it. A nasty-looking blue steel Ruger automatic. Looked like a thirty-eight caliber. He was holding it with the casual familiarity of a carpenter gripping an electric drill. Tool of the trade.

"Well," Bobinet said, "I don't believe her. Neither does my pal, here. Neither does Stockton the insurance guy."

"What's he doing in Hannibal?" Nudger asked, staring at the black bore of the automatic. Lord, he hated guns! Hated them and feared them.

The skeleton spat out a wheezy laugh. "What's this shit? You don't answer our questions, we answer yours? Like some kinda TV no-brainer game show where we take turns?"

"If it's a game show," Bobinet said, "it's 'Jeopardy!' "

The skeleton laughed again.

Bobinet said, "Stockton's got a vested interest in the diamonds, just like we do. He's the one tipped us about where you'd be going. Guy like that, he's got some wherewithal. Had a tap put on your girlfriend's phone and listened in when you called Marcy Lou here to check up on her. Figured out where she was from the conversation. We wanted to meet with you, tell you about the wrapping paper and the doll, then drive up here together and settle this. You shoulda been more careful."

Nudger felt anger churn in his stomach along with fear. "The bastard cut a deal with you two."

"Sure. We give Stockton half the diamonds back, his company pulls off the investigation. Quits pressuring the law to stay on the hunt. Kinda thing's done all the time in our line of work, Nudger. Diamonds cause people to compromise. 'Course, he did make us promise not to hurt Marcy Lou here."

"Decent of him." *And naive.* Nudger knew Stockton would never see the glitter of a single diamond. Bobinet and the skeleton would consider him a loose end and a risk. They'd kill him and keep everything for themselves. After they'd . . . done what they were going to do to Nudger and Marlou. After Marlou talked.

"Why'd you need me for this?" he asked. "How come you didn't just drive up here and find Marlou by yourselves?"

Bobinet said, "We think she mighta given the diamonds to you for safekeeping. Or at least you know where they are. Thing is, we wanted the matter settled once and for all, what with the police looking for us over snuffing Vanita."

"Not to mention Ed Franks."

"Not to mention."

The little car seemed to close in on Nudger. The skeleton's ragged breathing seemed louder. The air thicker and staler. Nudger's heart was dancing against his ribs, protesting lack of oxygen. His stomach was cold with terror. He might very soon have no need for oxygen. He didn't want to die. Not yet. Not for years.

Bobinet suddenly held a knife in his left hand. Lightly and expertly. He grabbed Marlou's chin abruptly with his right hand, squeezing it and grinning into her face. Her lips scrunched together and made her resemble a fish. She wasn't blinking; the fish was unafraid and mad as hell.

"Time to play 'Tell the Truth,' bitch," he said, "or I start slow with this blade and finish fast."

Her body gave a sudden, enraged jerk and she began slapping at him with the Raggedy Ann doll. "Go aheah an' kill me!" she shouted through her distorted lips. "You ain't gonna bewieve me anyways!"

Shocked, Bobinet released her chin and tried to draw back, but there was no way he could escape in the tiny car. He flicked backhanded at Marlou with the knife but his wrist hit the rearview mirror and the knife fell to the floor. The mirror was knocked at a cockeyed angle that caused Nudger to be staring into his own wide, frightened eyes.

"Wring your fucking neck!" Bobinet said, and squirmed around to try to get his hands on Marlou's throat. She kept hitting him with the doll. Over and over. Interfering with his vision. Stuffing flew from the doll's torn chest cavity and filled the car with floating shreds of batting. One of Bobinet's futile defensive grabs tore off Raggedy Ann's arm. More batting flew.

The skeleton sneezed, then began a horrible rattling cough.

"Shoot the cunt!" Bobinet commanded. "Don't kill her, though!"

The skeleton started to raise the blue steel automatic, but Nudger grabbed his wrist. Circled his fingers completely around almost fleshless bone.

But the skeleton was strong. He lashed out at Nudger with his free hand and missed, but his angular elbow bounced off Nudger's forehead. *Yeowch!* Hurt! Made Nudger mad.

The little car was rocking. Batting was flying thicker in the hot air. The skeleton was gasping. Sputtering and coughing uncontrollably. Nudger held on to the wrist of his gun hand, keeping the automatic aimed away from Marlou.

"Shoot the cunt!" Bobinet yelled again. He'd managed to get one hand to Marlou's throat and had her head back, squeezing. She continued to flail away with Raggedy Ann.

Hanging onto the skeleton's wrist, Nudger used his other arm and encircled Bobinet's neck, pulling him back hard toward the rear of the car. Bobinet actually growled in rage and frustration. Nudger wouldn't be able to hold him long.

"Get out," Nudger moaned to Marlou. "Get outa the car and run!"

"He's got a hold of me!" Marlou yelled. "Won't let loose!"

The skeleton wheezed and went into a coughing fit, his thin body wracked with spasms. The wrist jerked uncontrollably in Nudger's hand, like that of a marionette worked by a madman.

The skeleton's finger involuntarily twitched on the trigger.

Nudger's ears rang from the explosion in the confines of the compact car. A perfect round hole appeared in the front seat back. He felt Bobinet stiffen, then go limp.

When Nudger released him, Bobinet stared in childlike wonder as his head lolled back and to the side. Through the buzzing reverberations of the shot, Nudger heard Marlou say, "Gawd, the blood!"

The skeleton was still coughing, thrashing and struggling to catch his breath. Sucking in more floating cotton batting from the doll and making things worse. His left hand clawed for the door handle.

Found it.

Marlou was out of the car. Nudger helped the skeleton fall out on the other side by kicking at him as he released the wrist of his gun hand. Then he fumbled with the lock and door handle on his side and spilled from the little car. He landed on his hands and knees on the pavement. Something sharp dug into the heel of his hand.

From the other side of the car he could hear the skeleton still coughing and gasping. Even so the gun came into sight at the other end of the backseat and was waved in the general direction of Nudger. He slammed the miniature car door and scrambled to his feet. Grabbed Marlou's elbow and led her away. He was careful to keep the car between them and the skeleton. It was only a matter of time before the bony killer would regain control and be after them.

"That one goon dead?" Marlou asked beside Nudger. She was breathing almost as hard as the skeleton.

"Hope so," Nudger said.

"So much blood . . ."

"Better his than ours."

"Where we goin', Mr. Nudger?"

Pertinent question.

Nudger noticed there were people around them now. Apparently the car had muffled the shot enough so it didn't draw anyone's attention, parked as it was in a relatively desolate spot, a graveled area off Front, the street that ran parallel to the river.

He yanked Marlou along beside him and said, "We gotta keep folks around us so the skeleton won't try anything. So we'll be safe. You understand?"

"Heck, yeah!" She brushed cotton batting from her clothes. "But you really think that skinny one with the gun'll, like, come after us?"

"He'll come after the diamonds," Nudger said.

Marlou held on to the straw purse she'd automatically grabbed as she clambered from the car. Women and purses. She'd lost the matching straw hat, though. "I ain't *got* the diamonds."

"Tell him, not me," Nudger said. "But for now, calm down and act normal."

"Ain't gonna be easy."

"What about any of this has been?"

They'd been moving toward the river and were in with the throng of people boarding the *Mark Twain* at the foot of Center Street. Nudger paid for two tickets and led Marlou onto the sharply angled gangplank.

The riverboat was the most immediate if not the fastest way to leave town, and it would be crowded with tourists who'd provide safety in numbers.

As they trod across the gangplank he glanced back. Down along the sun-washed riverbank. He couldn't see the skeleton.

But he knew he was there somewhere, with death in his soul and greed in his eye.

And a gun in his pocket.

31

On board the boat, Nudger led Marlou to a bar where he bought them each a Coke. He wished he could have made his drink a stiff scotch and water, but he didn't want anything muddling his thinking. Besides, his stomach was twitching and was in no mood to accept hard liquor without violent protest.

He ushered Marlou to the open third deck, where there were some tiny square black tables and beige plastic chairs. They sat down. Sipped their drinks. Looked at each other.

Marlou said, "Jesus, Mr. Nudger!" The aftermath of action, what they'd just lived through, was finally washing over her. She began to tremble.

"Take it easy," Nudger said. "You might still need some strength." In the corner of his vision he saw the skeleton boarding the boat, slouching along the gangplank. His sleazy checked sport jacket was buttoned, no doubt to conceal the gun tucked in his belt.

Marlou spotted him. "Mr. Nudger—"

"I see him. He can't do anything in the middle of all these

people. Not on a boat there's no way off except for a long swim to shore. He doesn't look very athletic to me.''

The boat's whistle blasted twice, causing Nudger to jump. His nerves were still frayed. Down below, engines revved up like slumbering monsters awakened; the boat throbbed. Lines were loosed, and the riverbank seemed to move away from the rail.

The *Mark Twain* smoothly picked up speed. It traveled surprisingly fast. Nudger could hear the rush of water and see the brown-and-white churning expanse of river kicked up by the flailing paddle wheel; a long, tumultuous wake that fanned wide toward opposite banks. Nineteenth-century river pilots had seen the same sight, felt the same vibrations. Riverboat gamblers.

Someone was standing close behind Nudger. Marlou was staring up at whoever it was, over Nudger's shoulder.

Bill Stockton sat down at the table, between Nudger and Marlou. "I'll join you, if you don't mind."

"Or if we do," Nudger said. He was glad again to be surrounded by strangers; the protective herd that foiled predators.

The skeleton walked over and sat down opposite Stockton, letting out a wheezy sigh.

No one spoke to him. The skeleton said, "I'm sure Roger's dead."

"You shot him," Nudger said.

"You made me."

Stockton said, "Shut up. The diamonds are what we wanna talk about here."

"I'm sick of hearing about those diamonds," Marlou said.

Stockton grinned at her. He looked more than ever like a fat bird, Nudger thought. A pigeon. Nudger sure hated pigeons.

The skeleton stared hard at Marlou. He wheezed and blinked. "We want them diamonds in the worst way, miss. And this boat's gotta dock sometime."

Marlou took a long sip of soda from Nudger's cup, then shoved her chair back. Her face was flushed again, her green eyes narrowed. She was working up anger, maybe to counter her fear. "You all make me wanna just, like, scream!" she said.

That possibility seemed to alarm the skeleton. He sat up straighter.

But she didn't scream.

Surprised Nudger, though.

She said, "Okay. You was right all along. I got the diamonds. But I wasn't in on stealing them the first time nor the second. My sister got them in the mail from Rupert and brought them to me to hide, so they wouldn't be in her apartment. We bought a Raggedy Ann doll, just like the one I had when I was a little girl, and put them inside."

"Where are they now?" Stockton asked. He was leaning forward over the table, pinpoints of blue light in his eyes.

Marlou stood up, clutching her straw purse tight to her side. "Here!" she said. She reached into the purse, then turned away and strode to the rail. Drew back her arm like a major league pitcher.

Whipped it up and forward.

Nudger heard Stockton gasp. The skeleton said, "Jesus, no—"

The diamonds flew skyward and caught every ray of the evening sun. Glittered as they scattered and described a graceful, fateful arc to disappear into the churning river behind the boat.

"Aw, fuck . . ." the skeleton said, moaning. "Stupid cunt! Stupid cunt!"

Stockton was slumped back in his chair now, his face pale. "My God, girl! Almost a million dollars . . ."

"Maybe we can send down divers," the skeleton suggested. He was calmer but visibly devastated. Still staring out at the wide and timeless river that had claimed the diamonds and his dreams.

Stockton shook his head. "We're in the middle of the fucking Mississippi. It's deep here, and the water's always churning the soft bottom mud. It'd cost a fortune to dredge for the diamonds, and we might not recover even one. They could be washed a mile downstream by the time we even got an operation under way. Spread all over and buried deep in the silt." He glared at Marlou, who'd returned to stand next to the table, with pure rage and hate. "You realize what you've done, you country hick fool?"

Nudger said, "She did what you forced her into. It's over now. There are no more diamonds to chase, unless you're a fish."

The skeleton said, "It was gonna be my last big score. Money for what little time I got left."

"There's always Medicare," Nudger said, actually trying not to feel sorry for the wasted thief and killer.

"Fuck you, Nudger!" The skeleton stood up. He spat a yellow glob of phlegm on the deck in the general direction of Marlou, then stalked away.

Stockton sighed like a dying man giving up a last breath. He said, "Well, I took a run at it."

He flashed Nudger a sad smile. Even managed one for Marlou. Then he rose from the table and followed the skeleton toward the bow of the boat.

Marlou sat back down. Nudger didn't look at her. He sat and watched the trees on the bank sliding past. Their top branches were catching the setting sun; the leaves looked silver.

He heard Marlou shove her chair back and stand up. She said, "I wanna be alone now. Okay?"

He nodded.

She walked away, losing herself like the other two in the crowd on the boat.

Nudger knew she was in no danger now. There was nothing to be gained by harming her. Stockton's company, Sloan Trust Insurance, wasn't in the business of revenge. Neither was a pro like the skeleton. A loss was a loss.

Nudger had about broken even. Most of the retainer paid to him by Vanita had been used for expenses. That was no way to stay in business, he told himself. No way to avoid a court date with Eileen and Henry Mercato.

It was all so depressing.

He continued to sit there in the cooling evening, watching the bank slide past while he finished his soda and then chewed the cracked ice.

A pain shot through the right side of his jaw. Something small and sharp was lying on the edge of his tongue. He was sure he'd broken a tooth on the hard chunks of ice.

Gingerly he extended his tongue and squeezed the tiny object on it between thumb and forefinger. Removed it from his mouth and held it out and examined it.

It wasn't a fragment of tooth.

It looked like ice, but it wasn't.

It was clear and cold but much harder than ice.

32

Nudger saw that Marlou's paper cup was missing from the table. A handful of ice, not diamonds, had been flung over the rail and caught the sun. Disappeared in the deep muddy river. Marlou must have dropped the single diamond into Nudger's cup when she'd pretended to sip his drink by mistake. Then she'd slipped her own cup into her purse as she turned toward the rail. Pretended to dig in her purse for the diamonds. And then . . .

A handful of ice. Melting as it fell.

Nothing but ice!

Nudger sat on the gliding riverboat, the riverbank easing past like slow time. He stared at the diamond in his sweaty palm and felt its power. *People killed for these.* It was slightly smaller than a pea, clear but with a brilliant blue light in its center like a cruel soul. He had no idea of its quality. What it was worth. No idea what he should do with it. What he should do about Marlou. Naive but wily country girl, sensing a friend in the river. Like Huck, using it as a means of escape.

He knew he didn't want to see the skeleton use the diamonds to finance comfortable declining months bought with other lives.

Didn't want to see Stockton get the diamonds. His company, Sloan Trust, must have okayed his deal with known thieves and killers so the insurance loss would be halved. Better to be partners in crime than to look at a drastically reduced bottom line. So much for business ethics.

The merchants who were victims of the theft should have the diamonds back, but they'd be just as well off with the insurance settlement from Sloan Trust. Probably better. And it gave Nudger perverse satisfaction to know Sloan Trust would have to pay full coverage.

The river rolled with his thoughts. The steady vibration of the boat's engines throbbed through his body like temptation itself. *There's no such thing as innocence where money's concerned. Just people who haven't had the opportunity. Diamonds cause people to compromise.* He'd spent almost the entire thousand dollars Vanita had paid him as a retainer. Wasn't he owed something for his time and trouble? For risking his neck? No doubt that was what Marlou had in mind when she'd slipped him the diamond. She *wanted* him to have it. And she had to trust him to be silent, not to reveal what she'd done. She'd taken a chance on him. One she hadn't had to take. Gutsy move by a gutsy lady who paid her debts.

Debts.

A waitress wandered over to where Nudger was sitting near the rail. She had blond hair. Pale blue eyes exactly the color of the center of the stone in Nudger's hand.

She smiled at him. He ordered a scotch and water.

The murky water burbled past the hull, and stars began to sparkle in the darkening sky, like diamonds.

33

It was very dark when the boat docked in Hannibal. Bobinet's body had been discovered in the parked car. Between black shapes of buildings Nudger could see red lights flashing, intermittent silhouettes of a crowd.

The passengers disembarked in an orderly fashion, but fast. Maybe to see about the commotion up the bank toward town. Nudger didn't see Marlou, Stockton, or the skeleton in the crowd spilling down the gangplank, and he didn't look for them.

He played it straight. He walked slowly to the murder scene and to a heavyset man in jeans and a white shirt with a badge that said he was chief of police. Nudger explained more or less what had happened. What Marlou had done with the diamonds would be in Stockton's report anyway, a matter of record. Marlou hadn't been in on the original theft. She'd be in some trouble, but not much. Concealing evidence, and whatever charge might be attached to hurling the diamonds overboard—something she'd had to do to save her life. He figured her for probation.

More questions.

A signed statement.

Nudger went through the routine with a kind of weary patience. The Hannibal police and the Highway Patrol were looking for the skeleton, but Nudger was sure they wouldn't find him. It didn't matter much. The skeleton would die poor and in the not very distant future.

Stockton they'd locate. Or he'd come to them with his story. He'd keep himself on the right side of the law and complete his job so he could write his report for Sloan Trust.

Nudger left a few things out of his statement. He didn't mention that Marlou still had the diamonds.

Or that one of them was wrapped in a Kleenex deep in his pocket.

A month later he sold the diamond out of town to a legitimate jeweler for five thousand dollars. Since it wasn't mounted, there was no way it could be linked to the theft in New York; it might have been from his mother's wedding ring.

Nudger used the money to pay the back alimony he owed, which should keep Eileen and Henry Mercato at bay for at least six months. Eileen couldn't believe it at first. She seemed resentful that she couldn't haul him back into court. When he was finished paying off the rest of his debts, he still had a thousand dollars.

He used that and some of his Visa credit to buy a headstone for Vanita's grave. The one he chose from the mortuary's slick catalog wasn't his style, but it was a fancy one he was sure she would have liked. Italian red marble.

It was supposed to be an angel in flight, but when Nudger drove to the cemetery and saw it, he thought it looked more like an airplane.